CW01455688

Tales of Scotland Yard:
Lestrade

by Bianca Jenkins

© Copyright 2020 Bianca Jenkins

The right of Bianca Jenkins to be identified as the author of this work has been asserted by her in accordance with the Copyright, Designs and Patents Act 1998.

All rights reserved. No reproduction, copy or transmission of this publication may be made without express prior written permission. No paragraph of this publication may be reproduced, copied or transmitted except with express prior written permission or in accordance with the provisions of the Copyright Act 1956 (as amended). Any person who commits any unauthorised act in relation to this publication may be liable to criminal prosecution and civil claims for damage.

All characters appearing in this work are fictitious or used fictitiously.
Except for certain historical personages, any resemblance to real persons, living or dead, is purely coincidental. The opinions expressed herein are those of the authors and not of
Orange Pip Books.

Paperback ISBN 978-1-78705-720-3
ePub ISBN 978-1-78705-721-0
PDF ISBN 978-1-78705-722-7

Published by Orange Pip Books
335 Princess Park Manor, Royal Drive, London, N11 3G
www.orangepipbooks.com

Cover design by Brian Belanger

One

Try as he might, Inspector Johnson could no longer ignore the boy. Standing primly in the midst of chaos in what was most likely a brand new suit and seemingly unfazed by the crowd swarming around him, the young man would have blended in with the common criminal element present in the room had it not been for two things: the aforementioned suit, and the fact that he was somehow cleaner than the majority of the police force at Scotland Yard. Not, Johnson admitted to himself, that that was necessarily a particularly impressive feat in and of itself.

The fact that he had been here since shortly after the inspector had come in this morning, and had remained in place without so much as shifting position – as far as Johnson could tell based on the four times he had passed through the room and noticed the other man out of the corner of his eye – made Johnson wonder what exactly had brought him here, though he was equally if not more interested in what had caused him to stay.

Johnson made his way over to the desk sergeant to make an inquiry. Crane, a heavy-lidded man with thin lips and a sallow complexion, had a way of making his skin crawl without so much as uttering a word. Of course, when he did speak it was so much worse. Johnson usually tried to avoid the toad when he could, but unfortunately there was little he could do this time without simply approaching the lad himself and demanding an explanation.

He leaned almost casually against Crane's desk and found himself reconsidering as the man's dark eyes drifted up almost lazily to meet his. Stifling a sigh, he forced himself into the conversation.

"Snappy dresser," he commented, tilting his head ever so slightly. Crane did not bother to look. "Clean, too."

"Hmm," the other man hummed noncommittally. "Won't last," he pronounced judgment. Johnson felt his forehead wrinkle.

"New constable?" he asked, but that wasn't right. The boy would have been in a uniform.

"Former. Promoted. Came over from Fleet Street." Crane was no longer interested in either the newcomer or in the inspector invading his desk space. "Superintendent said to stick him with the first inspector to ask about him, if he didn't get fed up and leave first."

Johnson bit back an oath. "And I'm the first?" There was no need to ask. The very reason he had ignored the lad the first several times was that he had not wanted to deal with him.

Crane smiled up at him almost maliciously. This time Johnson did swear. Without another word he stalked across the room.

Up close the boy was not as young as Johnson had thought, but still young enough. His clothes *were* new, well-made, and a little more expensive than most Inspectors went for, but perhaps that was an attempt to offset his physical appearance: short, thin, dark-haired, and with a pinched look that on the street would make a man reconsider the safety of his wallet. Johnson paused in front of him and waited.

The young man met his gaze slowly. He had to look up to do so, and Johnson found himself staring down into the darkest pair of eyes he had ever seen in his life. The lad blinked – Johnson could not entirely shake his first impression of a boy standing untouched by all around him – and whatever might have been read in those almost black eyes by someone caught less off guard, shuttered. His expression closed to a polite mask.

Johnson wavered between curiosity and annoyance. "What's your name, boy?" He asked more sharply than he meant.

Perhaps exactly as sharply as he meant. He really had no interest in being followed around by some freshly promoted inspector that the superintendent clearly did not want around.

"Lestrade, sir," a brisk response, "Inspector Lestrade," he added carefully. It sounded as if it were the first time he had tried the title out. Johnson wondered how he liked it.

"Inspector Johnson," he introduced himself. "Seen the superintendent yet?"

"No, sir,"

"Well, you won't. Not unless you stick around long enough for him to notice you. Until that happens, or you quit or die, you're with me."

"Yes, sir," Not one for conversation, but maybe he was just nervous. Johnson wondered if Lestrade's polite expression would falter, just a bit, if he smacked him.

"Come on, then," Johnson headed back to his office, wondering just what exactly he was supposed to do with a rookie inspector. Paperwork, maybe?

"Yes, sir," That was going to get old quick.

"You don't need to speak unless you're answering a question," Johnson suggested, and the lad fell mercifully silent and followed him down the hall.

He looked around as they entered his office and realized he was further behind on his paperwork than he had originally thought. His office was in worse shape as well. It was both impressive and infuriating when the rookie took in the room and its contents without the slightest change of expression.

"Can you read, boy? Write?"

"Yes, sir."

"Which?"

"Both, sir."

Johnson pointed to a stack of cases heaped on a chair in the corner. "You can start by sorting through those and getting them in some sort of order. They go in that cabinet when you're finished."

Lestrade blinked at him, then looked back at the chair. Johnson wondered if he were going to argue with him, but he only asked, "Any special way you want them ordered, sir?"

The older inspector shook his head. "Just make sure I can find something when I need it." He doubted the lad would get far, or that anything he did would be particularly useful later, but at least it would keep him out of Johnson's way while he tried to catch up on his reports.

He sat down at his desk. Out of the corner of his eye he watched Lestrade gingerly examine the file sitting on the top of the stack. The lad's eyes furrowed as he stared down at the page, and a frown slipped through the mask.

"You did say you could read?" Johnson pressed. He received no reply, but Lestrade's eyes were moving across the page, albeit slowly. The older man left him to it and turned his attention to his own work.

Three-quarters of the way down the page his office door opened. A head poked through the now open door frame. "The lad's gone – Smith will be so disappointed. He was sure the boy would be waiting there all day and …" Inspector Adams stopped as he noticed the room's second occupant. "Yours?"

"It is now," Johnson grumbled. Lestrade never looked up. "Rookie inspector. Fresh from Fleet Street."

"He involved in that incident with the barber?" Adams grinned. "Are you going to introduce us now or wait a couple of weeks to see if he lasts?"

Johnson strangled a laugh into a cough and set down his report. "Inspector Lestrade."

The boy looked up and barely stopped himself. Johnson could still hear it. *"Yes, sir?"*

"This is Inspector Adams."

Lestrade sized up the other Inspector in much the same way a pickpocket on the street might. It lasted only a second, but nonetheless left both inspectors unsettled. "Pleased to meet you, sir." His voice was every bit as carefully pleasant as his expression.

"Well, we'll see," Adams returned. "Lestrade, was it?"

"Yes, sir."

Adams chuckled. "And Johnson has you doing his dirty work."

Something flashed in those eyes, but Lestrade's expression only shifted to mild uncertainty. "Sir?" he asked, his gaze drifting momentarily down to the file in his hand before returning to meet Adam's.

The inspector shook his head. "Never mind. I'm sure Johnson is only trying to make sure you're fully prepared for *every* aspect of your new position."

Eyes flickered between the two older men, and Lestrade must have realized some sort of response was in order. "Of course, sir."

"He's polite enough," Adams said a moment later, as the lad went back to sorting through the stack of files.

"Doesn't say much," Johnson grumbled. "Mostly variations of what you just heard. He *does* know his own name, at least. And he can read."

"That's something," Adams conceded. Excusing himself with a wave he added, "Smith will probably be by later to size him up."

By the time Smith showed up Johnson had made it through the last of his reports and was entertaining himself by watching the rookie inspector sort through a vastly diminished stack of files. Around him, and seemingly with no particular design or method were a number of smaller piles, and Lestrade had even gone so far as to open one of the cabinet drawers. Now he stood frozen, halfway through some turn that he had started but not completed, his head tilted slightly and his eyes startlingly unfocused.

Whatever had caught his attention had caused a complete change in the man; his body suddenly seemed to radiate an almost nervous energy. Fascinated, Johnson did not immediately notice when the other inspector invited himself inside.

Smith cleared his throat and nudged the foot of other man's desk with the toe of his shoe. "Working hard, I see."

7

Johnson recovered and rolled his eyes. "Lestrade," he snapped, and was gratified when the young man started. The next instant he had recovered completely and was waiting for one of the other two to make the first move. Johnson sighed. "This is Inspector Smith. Smith, this is the rookie."

"Inspector Lestrade," Smith greeted the other man. Lestrade's response was entirely predictable.

"Yes, sir. Pleased to meet you."

"And you," Smith replied, amused. "Learning anything useful?"

Uncertain again, Lestrade blinked. "Sir?"

Smith laughed outright. "You always this polite, rookie?" He asked, smiling in an attempt to reassure the lad.

Lestrade hesitated, and Johnson wondered what was going on behind those carefully neutral eyes. "I try, sir," he said at last.

Smith snorted. "Never mind the 'sir,' rookie."

"Yes, Inspector."

Johnson sighed again. He could feel a headache coming on.

"Smith will do." Predictably, Smith's humor never wavered. Looking over at Johnson, he asked, "Want me to take him for a walk? Give you a break?"

Johnson stood. "We could both use a break," he admitted. "Come on, rookie. Let's see how you do on the street." Lestrade considered his unfinished assignment only briefly before nodding.

"Fleet Street, huh?" Smith asked as they turned a corner and Scotland Yard disappeared behind them. He was slightly ahead of the young man, but did not miss the way Lestrade's eyes flickered toward him for less than a second.

"Yes, sir." Smith figured the response was reflex by now and ignored it.

"How long?"

"Five years," Lestrade replied promptly. "A year with the River Police before that."

Smith let out a low whistle. "You don't look near old enough for that," he said easily. Lestrade shrugged; as polite as he had been so far, he apparently felt little need to explain himself. Smith waited to see what he would do, but he seemed to feel no need to break the silence either.

"Any family?" Johnson did *not* care for the extended pause.

Lestrade hesitated. Both men saw him do it. "My sister lives here in London with me." His voice was tight.

Smith and Johnson exchanged a glance. "Anyone else?" The latter pressed, interested. Here was something that threatened the polite young inspector that had spent the last few hours sorting files without complaint. Something glimmered in his eyes, as yet undefined.

"Our mother died when we were small," he replied dutifully. One more question, Johnson decided, just to see what would happen.

"Anyone else? Father? Brother?" Lestrade flinched.

"Not in London," he said darkly, and Johnson left it at that.

The man was clearly not comfortable talking about his family. It was to his credit that he had chosen to do so anyway instead of lie, Johnson supposed.

Smith tilted his head as the sound of a police whistle cut through the air. "Not far," he guessed, "two blocks over?"

"Willie's," Johnson groaned. Smith turned and smiled at the rookie.

"Want to go break up a bar fight?" He asked, and was gratified when Lestrade's eyes widened ever so slightly. The lad was a tricky read unless you caught him completely off guard.

"At Willie's?" His voice dropped to almost a whisper, and Smith laughed.

"Got to get your feet wet sometime!" He declared cheerfully. Johnson scowled.

"If he gets killed they'll blame me," he pointed out as they started toward the bar.

Lestrade did not get killed. The first person to come after him took a blow to the chin that left both inspectors impressed in spite of themselves as his head snapped sharply back and he fell to the floor senseless.

It was a lucky shot; Lestrade's attacker had not been expecting much of a fight from his much smaller opponent. The man he had been sparring with before the inspectors had so rudely interrupted took a different approach. He threw a chair.

Lestrade turned and the worst of the impact jolted down his shoulder and upper arm. He staggered back, and there the two older inspectors lost sight of him as they were drawn into the fray. Belatedly both realized that this was less of a fight and more of an all-out brawl, and that perhaps they should have left the rookie outside.

Someone slammed Johnson into a table; he thought he caught a glimpse of Lestrade being lifted off the ground as he went down. *"I've gotten that boy killed,"* he had time to think as he crashed through the table and kept going. If he ended up in the floor he was as good as dead; they would trample him and never know he was there.

Someone jerked him roughly away from the still overturning table and to his feet. He stumbled trying to regain his balance, dimly aware that there was blood running into his eyes. He staggered into Adams, who was giving him some sort of look.

"Where's the kid?" he shouted over the din around them. Johnson shook his head stupidly and Adams rolled his eyes. "Pull yourself together, Henry!"

Johnson shook his head and looked around, trying to get his bearings. Reinforcements had arrived, and he could already see that the melee would be over shortly. Smith had backed himself against a wall intentionally and was keeping his opponent at an arm's length. Flint, clearly off-duty based on the way he was dressed, was near the bar; Johnson watched him smash a beer bottle across some poor drunk's face. Lestrade was nowhere in sight.

The fight was over now, as swiftly as it had probably begun. Drunks and slightly-less-than-sober participants from the brawl were slinking out the door, leaving constables and inspectors in their wake, some freshly arrived and still ready for a fight, others all but collapsing into the nearest available seating. Johnson scanned the bar, still searching for his erstwhile rookie and hoping he had not, as he feared, gotten the man killed on his first day as an inspector.

Smith reappeared, scowling at his chest. Someone had bloodied his nose and the resulting spray had stained his jacket, tie, and shirt, but Johnson had been there that morning when Adams had told him the light beige suit was a bad idea – what if he got blood on it? The man had been warned, but even without the friendly admonition he should have known better. Blood aside, it was nearly impossible to keep clean on the job.

Adams had sliced open the back of his hand on something, likely while hauling Johnson up off the floor – the man was incredible in a fight. Nearly untouchable, he seemed to weave through a crowd as if it were nothing more than a minor inconvenience. He seemed not to have noticed the cut yet as he scanned the bar, and Johnson realized they were both looking for the same person.

Licking his lips to moisten them, Johnson swallowed. "Lestrade!" he barked. His throat spasmed, and he told himself it was the fight and not fear that left his mouth so dry. Looking around once more helplessly, he tried again. He could not ignore Adams' glare as it skewered him from across the room.

"Sir?" The weary response reached him. He spun around too fast and the room shifted. He put a hand out to steady himself and found nothing.

Instead of falling he slammed into a slight but surprisingly solid frame. Lestrade rocked slightly at the impact but held steady. Johnson righted himself almost immediately after and stared down at the decidedly still-alive rookie before him. The younger man held out a spotless white handkerchief to him; Johnson considered it for a moment.

"You're bleeding, sir," Lestrade finally said, gesturing with the handkerchief, and Johnson remembered that his own blood was still dripping into his eyes and accepted the other inspector's offering. He wiped the blood from his eyes first, then pressed the cloth to his forehead.

"Thank you," he said gruffly. "I see you're still alive."

"Yes,"

"Are you hurt?" Johnson asked, and for the second time that day, Lestrade hesitated. This time the older man did not wait to see what he would say. "Where?"

Lestrade stiffened, but he answered anyway. "My shoulder and arm are stiff."

"The chair," Johnson thought.

"Someone tried to cut me open," Lestrade gestured, and the other Inspector could see the cut in his jacket, but whatever the material, the knife had been stopped there. "When that didn't work his friend kicked me in the back of the leg. Might be some bruising later..." The lad had been lucky.

"You could have been killed." Johnson had not meant to snap, but it told him more than he cared to admit that Lestrade's expression instantly blanked and his posture immediately straightened. His response did nothing to help.

"Yes, sir," he agreed blandly. A beat, then he added, "My apologies."

Johnson shook his head at the man and immediately regretted it. "Not your fault," he said. "I should never have let you get involved in something like this on your first day.

"Like it or not," he thought, *"you're my responsibility."*

"You did well though. You obviously know how to handle yourself somewhat or you wouldn't be standing here now."

14

Lestrade grimaced. "With all due respect, sir, I'd much rather be sitting right now."

Johnson blinked at him through vision that was starting to blur a little bit. "Good god, Lestrade. Sit down."

Lestrade obliged, swinging a chair around with his left hand and perching almost prissily on the edge of it. He settled uncomfortably, and Johnson guessed his back was bothering him as well and would not have let him fully relax even had he wanted to. Johnson himself was starting to ache in various places he had not realized had taken a beating.

Johnson found his own seat, unable for the moment to do more. Someone else could worry about questioning constables and figuring out what had started the fight in the first place. Someone who had shown up after the worst had broken up. Someone who didn't care and would probably just sweep the whole affair under the rug.

Truth be told, Johnson didn't really care either. Not about a tavern brawl. Not enough to put up a fuss. Not enough to risk crossing the wrong person.

A shadow fell across the floor in front of the inspector, and he leaned slightly to the right. It was not enough, but it was the most he could manage at the moment. The shadow's owner noticed and was kind enough to step around and into view.

It was none other than Willie, the tavern's robust owner and namesake. He catered to anyone and everyone, as long as they could pay, treated the police with cool indifference, and stayed out of the way if someone started a fight. "Don't get attached, don't get involved," was his motto, and so far it had kept him alive through several particularly rough patches.

He was smiling now, though, as he looked them both over. "All right there, Mr. Lestrade?" he asked, his tone far more friendly than Johnson could ever remember hearing. "You got that promotion, did ya? You in that suit and tagging along with the Inspectors Johnson and Smith all proper like."

"I did, thank you, Mr. Williams." Lestrade offered a polite smile that did nothing to hide the exhaustion in his eyes.

"Put up a good fight tonight," Willie, or Mr. Williams, added brightly. Johnson wondered what his Christian name was. Before tonight he had always assumed it was William. "Thought the fella with the knife might have done ya in."

Another smile, this one weary. "Not this time, I'm afraid." Lestrade looked down at his jacket ruefully.

"Aye, next time, maybe," Willie offered, as if they were discussing the weather rather than the inspector's possible death. "Anything I can get ya, Mr. Lestrade? Look about done in, if ya don't mind my saying so."

"Thank you, but no, Mr. Williams," Lestrade was pulling himself to his feet, "Another time, perhaps."

"Aye, certainly," Willie agreed as Johnson grumbled to his feet as well. "Good night, Mr. Lestrade, and to you, Inspector Johnson."

They stumbled across the bar to join Smith and Adams. "I didn't know he knew my name," Johnson mused, turning to watch the man as he righted tables and chairs with the ease that comes only with a great amount of practice. "And he certainly knows your name, *Mr. Lestrade.*"

Lestrade blinked. "He knows everyone's name, sir. And he never forgets a face."

"Good to know," Adams grumbled. "Let's get out of here, all right?"

"Rookie's alive," Johnson felt the need to point out. "Got hit by a chair and kicked in the back of the leg. His jacket kept a knife from spilling his guts all over the floor."

"He got lucky," Adams said.

"And Johnson learned not to take a rookie into a fight on his first day," Smith put in reasonably, as if he had had no part in the business. "Now let's go."

"Go home, Lestrade," Johnson waved the Inspector off. "You can finish the files tomorrow."

"Yes, sir," Lestrade said wearily, "Thank you, sir,"

They watched him go.

"He's certainly polite," Smith offered, rolling his shoulders back and cracking his neck.

Adams scowled. "It's an act," he declared. "A well-practiced act, likely fine-tuned after years of practice, but an act all the same."

Smith did not disagree. "Good luck getting him to drop it, if that's the case."

Two

Johnson was not surprised when he woke up late the next morning. His schedule for the past two weeks had been chaotic at best, and after the previous night's tavern-related expedition, it only made sense that something would have to give. His only real concern, as he dragged his aching body out of bed, was how his freshly promoted charge was likely faring in his absence. Standing in a corner somewhere, possibly, waiting for Johnson to show up or for someone else to take pity on him.

Lestrade had proved himself last night at least. He could have easily been killed, but instead had held his ground. And there had been a spark there, however briefly, suggesting that maybe Lestrade was not simply a prim-and-proper yes-man, but that he might become an inspector in his own right, someone to be reckoned with.

If he survived. And if the opportunity ever arose. There was little enough opportunity for mediocrity at Scotland Yard these days. Greatness was almost completely out of the question.

Johnson smiled bitterly as he dressed and made his way downstairs.

Johnson's office was cleaner than it had been since the inspector had moved in. The chair full of files was empty. A quick glance in the filing cabinet showed everything neatly stowed, and closer examination revealed a system of organization that seemed easy enough to manage. The inspector was pleasantly surprised.

Lestrade, however, was nowhere in sight. Johnson wondered if he had been abducted by one of the other inspectors. *"Dear god let it be Smith or Adams. Craddock will eat him alive."* He left his office to hunt down his wayward companion, the muscles in his shoulders and back complaining all the while.

He found Adams in his office, the cut on his hand from the night before well bandaged. Johnson noted that it was his right hand, and made a note to keep his distance. An injury on his right hand was going to make writing difficult for a while, which would in turn make the inspector himself downright unpleasant.

Adams looked up from his desk. "Looking for the rookie?" he taunted. Judging by the gleam in his eye Adams knew exactly where Lestrade was, but he looked like he needed cheering up, so Johnson let him have this one.

"Have you seen him?" He obliged.

Adams grinned. It was not a nice smile, but one mixed with irritation and a bit of distaste. "A woman got him," he told Johnson, "Some lady frantic about her little one she says had gone missing. Everyone else dodged her, but he couldn't say no. He doesn't have an office yet, so he escorted her to the kitchen, gentle as you please, to hear her story."

Johnson considered this. "You think he's soft?" he asked thoughtfully.

Adams shrugged. "Surely he knows by now that there's very little we can actually do..."

Another shrug. "Honestly, I'm surprised she even came in. It's not as if anyone really trusts us anymore." Adams studied his bandaged hand. "There may be some things your rookie doesn't know yet. I don't know *how* he doesn't, but he'd better learn quick."

Johnson sighed. "I'll go find him. He really shouldn't be handling cases on his own yet."

"Or breaking up bar fights," Adams called after him as he backtracked down the hall. The kitchen was not far from the inspectors' offices. It was also not much of a kitchen. There was a stove, and an ancient teapot that had been there longer than anyone currently at the Yard could remember. There were a few cracked communal teacups that were generally only used by newcomers until they remembered to bring their own.

Lestrade was there with a woman. He had found two chairs, somewhere, pathetic looking things but apparently sturdy enough. He had also made some tea and he had offered the woman the least battered of the communal cups. As he approached, Johnson could see that she sat staring down into it as she slowly rotated it in her hands, speaking slowly and tearfully while Lestrade sat across from her and wrote almost painstakingly in the notebook he had balanced on his knee.

It was obvious that the woman had been crying earlier, likely that she had been hysterical. Her eyes were red and swollen and her face was blotchy; one hand also held captive a severely abused handkerchief that Johnson guessed had once been Lestrade's. She was calm enough now, although her chin trembled slightly and her voice occasionally caught.

Inspector Flint stood just outside the doorway, watching the two with an intensity that made the hair prickle on the back of the other inspector's neck. Seeing Johnson, he offered a not-entirely-sincere grin and went about his business. Johnson wondered idly what the man's interest in the new inspector was, but pushed the thought aside for the time.

Instead of interrupting Johnson simply stood there, waving Lestrade on when he paused and looked up, smiling reassuringly at the lady when she did the same even though he knew this whole endeavor was simply an exercise in futility.

"Harold was a good boy. He could get into mischief sometimes, but he didn't mean it," the woman told Lestrade. "He really didn't mean it. And he smiled at everyone. Everyone! Such a friendly babe." Her chin trembled again, and this time she could not stop herself. The woman burst into tears once more.

Lestrade simply waited, either unwilling or unable to comfort her. It took only a few minutes for her to cry herself out, and when she at last sniffled and took another sip of tea – as if she had only just remembered its existence – he asked if she could think of anything else he might need to know.

She shook her head and sniffed again. "You *will* look for him?" she begged. "My own mother said it was hopeless, that I'd never see him again. And my husband doesn't think you'll even try...but you will, won't you? My Harold..." She dissolved once more into tears, sobbing frantically into an already drenched handkerchief.

"I'll try, Mrs. Abbot." Lestrade's voice, though low, cut through the woman's grief. "I cannot make any promises, but I will look for him. You have my word on that."

Johnson stifled a groan, but the effect the other inspector's words had on Mrs. Abbot was instantaneous. Her back straightened, her head lifted. She was again in control of herself, at least, for the moment. How long that would last...

He and Lestrade escorted the woman back to the front of the building and out into the street, where Lestrade called a cab for her. When she had bundled herself successfully inside and the cab driver had waved and started off down the road, Johnson turned to face the other inspector.

"What the hell do you think you are doing?" he demanded. Lestrade stood his ground.

"No one else would so much as speak with her," he explained, his polite tone at odds with the sudden stiffness in his shoulders.

"Because it's a lost cause," Johnson told him. Lestrade bristled, his back and shoulders going rigid, and Johnson stared at him. "You know that! You *have* to know that, Lestrade! Children disappear every day and are never seen again! They're stolen, or simply sold, or murdered by parents who can't afford them or don't want them! We can look and look and drive ourselves mad and still never find even a trace of them because no one will talk to us – no one trusts us – and it doesn't matter anyway because that child is gone!"

The other man's eyes flashed, then darkened even further, a feat Johnson would not have thought possible. Lestrade let out a long, deep sigh through his nose and took a step forward to stand directly in front of the older inspector.

"Someone had to hear what she had to say. Someone has to look for that boy. It doesn't matter if they find him or not. Someone still has to look." Lestrade spoke so softly that Johnson almost had to strain to hear him. There was something in the younger man's voice he could not quite identify, and it worried him.

"You? You'll drive yourself to an early grave that way, Lestrade." Johnson sighed. "When does it stop? When you find him? You might never find him. You could spend the rest of your life looking and still never find him. Or worse, you do find him. What then?" He became aware that Lestrade was trembling, though whether from anger or some other repressed emotion did not know.

"Surely you know the realities of our job." Johnson spoke more softly now. Almost gently. An image of the man in front of him shattering into pieces popped into his mind, and he clenched his fists. "You said six years. You can't still be this blind after six years."

Lestrade's shoulders slumped. "I know I won't find him," he admitted, his voice harsh as he met Johnson's gaze. Deep pools of black ink poured into the other man as if searching his soul. "That doesn't mean I don't have to look."

Johnson closed his eyes and rubbed his forehead. "You'll kill yourself, Lestrade." He warned hopelessly. The older inspector stared down at the man in front of him: small, sallow, with an air about him that made him seem not entirely trustworthy, and utterly and completely unable to walk away from a grieving mother and lost child.

"Where do you plan to start?"

Lestrade had the woman's address. Johnson hailed a cab and soon they were on their way. "You took notes on the interview?" When the other nodded, Johnson beckoned for him to hand the notebook over. Lestrade did so wordlessly. Johnson flipped the notebook open and frowned.

"I thought you said you could write. What the hell is this?"

Lestrade looked distinctly uncomfortable. "Shorthand, sir."

"Shorthand?" It did not look like any form of shorthand Johnson had ever seen before.

"I'm a slow writer, sir. This is faster." Lestrade admitted reluctantly, as if he expected some rebuke for the confession. Johnson felt his eyebrows raise.

"And you can read it?" When Lestrade nodded, he tossed the book back at him. "Then do so. Out loud, please."

Lestrade flipped the notebook open to the first page.

"Harold Abbot. Three years, seven months old. Blonde hair, blue eyes. Weight roughly thirty-two pounds, thirty-three inches in height. Missing front left tooth. Small scar over left eyebrow – fell and hit head on a chair about a year ago. Last seen Borough Market, Southwark Street, shortly before two in the afternoon. He was with the mother and her sister.

"According to Mrs. Abbot they make the trip almost weekly. He's never wandered off before. She said he didn't this time either. She simply looked down and he was gone."

Johnson rolled his shoulders and leaned back into the seat. "Any enemies? Anyone who might wish the boy harm? Or the parents?"

"No one she could think of. Said the boy was friendly to everyone."

"And everyone was friendly back?" Johnson asked.

"She seemed to think so," Lestrade admitted. "She also said everyone knew when they were going to the market. He told everyone he saw whenever they went. Family, employees, neighbors, complete strangers, the cab driver..."

"Not much to work with," Johnson grumbled. He hated this. "So what do you plan to do?"

"Confirm the details with the family. And with neighbors, if possible." Johnson scowled. *"Damn it, he knows they probably won't even speak with us and he's going to try anyway and likely get spit on for all his trouble."*

Lestrade continued, unaware of the other man's inner dialogue. "Try to retrace their steps on Southwark."

"Do you have a list of places they visited?" Lestrade nodded without looking up. *"Adams was right about him,"* Johnson thought, fascinated in spite of the situation.

Mr. Abbot would not so much as let them in the side door. Neither he nor anyone else in the household would speak with them. He might as well have slammed the door in their faces. Johnson turned to gauge the other man's reaction but the mask that had resurfaced the second the door opened was still firmly in place. There was no way of knowing how he felt about the conversation they had just had with the missing boy's father. Johnson figured he could probably guess anyway.

The neighbors were no more receptive than the father had been. Several refused to even answer the door. Johnson had yet to figure out how people could still tell they were the police even when dressed in plainclothes, but somehow they always seemed to know.

He looked at Lestrade and reconsidered. Lestrade was so obviously a plainclothesman that it almost hurt to look at him, but at the same time there was something about him that also suggested he was fully capable of stealing you blind if he took a notion to. Perhaps Lestrade tried so hard to look like a policeman because he was trying to avoid the alternative.

"Now what?" Johnson asked, trying to keep the aggravation out of his voice. It really was an excellent opportunity to see how the other inspector would carry out an investigation on his own, and so far Lestrade showed promise. It was also, unfortunately, likely to be an equally valuable opportunity to observe how the younger man handled frustration and failure on the job – sadly, one of the best indicators of whether or not someone would last in their line of work.

Lestrade was silent for a moment. "Maybe someone at the market saw something," he ventured at last, reaching for his notebook and flipping to a page with what looked vaguely like a list. "Someone at one of the stalls."

It was the next logical step, but Johnson wondered if it would matter. It was just as likely no one there would talk to them either. All the same, he hailed a cab and the two inspectors set off for Southwark Street.

Here at last they had a bit of luck. One of the vendors recognized Lestrade as a customer and greeted him cautiously, but it was by far the best response they had gotten so far. Others had realized they were with the Yard and immediately found themselves either far too busy or far too forgetful to be of use.

"Yes, Mr. – Inspector Lestrade," the vendor confirmed warily, "I know the mother and child." He was tall and thin, all sharp angles and long limbs, with pale green eyes that watered as he squinted down at them. "They come every week. Sometimes with the sister. Once the husband came with them."

Lestrade pulled out his notebook. "And the boy, did he ever wander off? Did he ever get distracted?"

The man shook his head. "He stayed right near her, Mr. Lestrade. Like a little shadow. Never strayed from her side." He shook his head. Pointing, he added, "She was right there when it happened. I heard a scream and looked up. She was there, and the sister, but the boy was gone."

Lestrade made a note. "What did you think about the boy? What sort of child was he?"

"Always smiling," the vendor smiled himself as he answered, "always happy. Always had something to say, though you couldn't always make sense of it, of course. But he'd babble away quite happily to anyone who would listen. I can't think of anyone who didn't look forward to his visits."

"Can you think of anyone who might have had something against the rest of the family?" Lestrade asked. "The mother? Or the sister? Even the father, perhaps?"

The vendor shook his head. "Can't think of a soul, Mr. Lestrade. Everybody loved that child, and that's the truth. Even if someone *did* have something against one of the family, I can't imagine them taking it out on that little boy."

Lestrade frowned at his notepad, thinking. "Thank you so much for your time, Mr. Richards," he said slowly, still staring at his notepad as if it held the answer to his current dilemma. Abruptly he looked back up at the man. "Can you think of anyone else who might be willing to talk to us? Anyone else who might know something?"

Richards scratched his head. "Maybe a couple might talk to you, but not anyone who might be able to help, Mr. Lestrade. I'm so sorry."

"That's quite all right, Mr. Richards," Lestrade closed his notebook with a snap and tucked it into his jacket pocket. "We appreciate your time."

The man nodded and excused himself to deal with a customer. Johnson watched him go, then turned to look back at Lestrade. "Well?" He asked.

Lestrade did not respond. He was staring at the empty space the vendor had previously occupied, his eyes not quite focused as he considered their next move. Johnson watched, waiting to see what the other man would decide.

Finally Lestrade shook his head, and his shoulders slumped. "I don't know," he admitted.

"You might try the hospital," Johnson suggested reluctantly. "Bit of a long shot, but worth a try if you have the time and inclination."

Lestrade shifted uneasily, but his back straightened, and he led the older detective back toward the street with renewed purpose.

Nobody at the hospital wanted to talk to them either. It took Lestrade the better part of an hour to finally get one of the nurses to stop long enough to speak with him, and during that time it became increasingly evident to Inspector Johnson that the other man would rather be anywhere other than their current location. The new inspector did *not* like hospitals.

To be fair, most of the people Johnson knew did not care for hospitals, and especially for being a patient in one, but for someone who was visiting, and that only in a professional capacity, it was quite clear that Lestrade was incredibly uncomfortable. Twitchy, almost, as if he half expected a team of doctors to appear, drag him into an operating room and start cutting him open, all while he was fully conscious. Johnson shook his head in disgust, wondering where his mind came up with these things.

The nurse reluctantly heard him out and agreed to check if any unidentified children had turned up. Telling them to wait right there, she turned and started down the hallway, swiftly disappearing from view.

"Think she'll come back?" Johnson asked, for lack of anything better to do, and also quite possibly to offer the rookie a distraction before his jaw shattered from the pressure he was putting on it.

Lestrade almost winced. "Said she would." He had forgotten to be polite again.

"Not a fan of hospitals?" the older Inspector asked, and this time Lestrade flinched. His eyes skirted up to meet Johnson's only to flit way at the last second. Opening his mouth to speak, he was cut off by a loud crash a couple of rooms down.

The man jumped. Paling, he stared in the direction of the clatter for several seconds before seeming to catch himself. Letting out a short breath through his nose, he shifted, regaining control of his body and his expression.

His eyes were still a bit wild as the rest of him settled back into some semblance of calm, and he was still far too tense. Johnson wondered what, exactly, had happened to him in the past to get him so worked up, and why he had come here, case or no case.

The nurse returned. "Three separate cases of children found, but none of them over a year old. Sorry, Inspector."

Lestrade managed a tight nod. "Thank you anyway, Miss," he said a bit stiffly. "We appreciate your time."

"You might try the morgue," the woman suggested tightly.

It was the next logical step, but Lestrade did not look happy about it. Johnson supposed he would have felt more strongly about it himself if he had not had the last ten years or so to get used to the idea.

Any tension that had bled out of the younger inspector's frame as they left the hospital returned in force as they approached the table on which lay the still form of a young boy. Johnson himself found it a bit much – knowing that this kind of thing happened all the time was completely different from seeing the tiny body laid out before him. Lestrade looked like he might shatter from the strain.

He examined the child carefully, almost reverently. Over his shoulder Johnson checked off each part of the description: height, age, hair, scar. The mortician confirmed eye color and the missing tooth. They had found the lost boy.

Johnson almost wished they hadn't. He wondered how Lestrade felt about it.

The younger inspector finished his examination and thanked the doctor. He was silent as they left, his eyes not quite focused as if his mind were elsewhere, his shoulders slightly hunched under his jacket. Johnson watched him carefully; while this kind of thing could offer a look into how a man might handle similar instances in the future, it could also easily break him, especially during his first days on the job.

Lestrade paused once they got out into the street and stood still, simply staring at nothing. Johnson waited, but as time stretched on he began to wonder whether the other inspector were even capable of pulling himself back from wherever he had gone. Reluctantly he cleared his throat.

"Lestrade?"

The man turned his head. Dark, empty eyes slowly began to focus and meet his. He closed his eyes for a long moment, then seemed to come back to himself. "I should let the mother know." He did not seem inclined to start moving again just yet.

Johnson sighed. "Do that. Then go home, Lestrade. The day's almost over anyway, and the paperwork can wait until tomorrow."

Lestrade started to frown. Catching himself, he nodded instead. His "Yes, sir," while still polite, was subdued. Turning, he started off down the street.

Johnson watched him go.

Three

"Solve the case?" Adams asked with false cheer as the other inspector entered Scotland Yard the next morning. Johnson scowled at him in reply.

"Boy dragged me all over London yesterday," he grumbled, ignoring Crane as they passed his desk. "Nobody wanted to talk to us. Missing child's own father wouldn't talk to us. And still he went on, up and down the street, all over the market, even to the hospital – and let me tell you, that boy does not like hospitals one bit."

Adams was curious. "No? Did you ask him why?"

Johnson shook his head. "Didn't want to know why. Doesn't matter anyway. Lestrade stood his ground. About jumped out of his shoes when somebody dropped something behind him, but he held it together, not that we got anything useful other than a suggestion to try the morgue."

Adams sighed and stopped to lean against the wall. "And?"

Johnson stopped as well. Shrugging, he stared off down the hall. "What do you think you would have done if you had found the corpse of a three-year-old boy at the morgue on your second day?"

Adams swore. "Think he'll be back?" he asked, and Johnson was forced to consider.

"Who'll be back?" As was typical for the man, Smith had arrived just in time to miss the story.

"Lestrade. They found the child he was looking for."

"Dead?"

Johnson nodded, and Smith looked thoughtful for a moment. "I don't know if I would come back after that, not if it had happened my first day."

"Second," Adams corrected. Smith rolled his eyes.

"I imagine a day or two makes little difference when it comes to something like that. Either way, he may well be made of stronger stuff."

"Maybe," Adams sounded doubtful. Johnson thought about the younger inspector's hunched shoulders and distracted gaze and did not feel much confidence in the matter. Lestrade had looked almost broken yesterday when they had parted ways.

Smith looked from one man to the other incredulously. "Johnson, he's in your office," he finally said. "There's no maybe about it. He came back."

Johnson started. "Really?" He shook his head. "I honestly wasn't sure, last night."

"Well he's there, and he didn't look particularly broken to me," Smith told him. "Maybe like there was something on his mind – got that distracted look he had on when I came in the other day."

Adams snorted and straightened up. "Well, he's still here, and that's what counts, I guess." He gave Johnson a pointed look. "Try not to get him killed or run him off?"

With that parting shot, he continued down the hall and ducked into his office.

Smith smiled after him. "Not a bad idea, if you can manage it," he quipped. "By the way, Flint was asking about the rookie yesterday. If I'd met him, what I thought of him, that kind of thing."

"He was watching Lestrade interview Mrs. Abbott, the boy's mother, when I found them." Johnson replied uneasily. "Wonder what he's after."

Smith shrugged. "Might just be curious. It's not every day a rookie tries to run an interview on his second day without his supervising inspector present." With that he departed, leaving Johnson to either stand aimlessly in the hall alone or head to his own office and deal with whatever was waiting for him in the form of the young inspector. After only a moment of debate, Johnson made his way down the hall.

"Sir," Lestrade was waiting for him, suit and tie immaculate as ever. He seemed to have pulled himself together after the events of the previous day, though it did not escape Johnson's notice that he seemed nervous.

"Lestrade," Johnson retaliated, not quite sure he was ready for whatever he sensed what coming his way. Lestrade nodded, then hesitated, as if unsure how to proceed. Johnson took pity on him. "What is it?"

Lestrade looked down for a moment, perhaps steeling himself, before asking, "Why would someone give a child opium?"

Johnson felt his eyebrows raise. "To get them to sleep. Or keep them quiet." He wondered how Lestrade didn't already know that, and then he wondered why the man was asking. Then he remembered that the doctor had mentioned something about the child they had found the night before having overdosed on opium.

"Probably the mother, or the sister, or the grandmother gave him some to settle him down and gave him too much. And then they didn't want to admit it. Or it could have been a maid or any other servant..." He wasn't sure what to do with the almost betrayed look that Lestrade could not quite manage to hide, and so he ignored it. "Let it go, Lestrade. It's over."

"The doctor said there were two more turned up last month same way. Little older, one was a girl, but both were blonde with blue eyes."

"Both overdosed on opium?"

Lestrade nodded.

"And you think they might be connected." Johnson was not asking. It wasn't a question. Lestrade answered anyway.

"I don't know. But the doctor thought it was worth mentioning."

Johnson let out a long breath and sat down. "Could be connected," he admitted, "Were the bodies identified?"

Lestrade shook his head. "I tried going through missing persons..." he trailed off, and Johnson stifled a sigh. Their missing persons file was a joke.

Drumming his fingers absently against the desk, Johnson tried to think back to the examination the night before. "No sign of injury on the boy...no bruising, no welts, no other sign of ill treatment. Whoever took him was being careful. They wanted him whole, and well, and..." Johnson felt his mouth go dry. He really hoped he was wrong about this. "Did the doctor mention any injuries on the other children?"

Lestrade shook his head. "He said they were clean as well." Johnson scowled at the younger man before him. The other inspector blinked. "Sir?"

"Nothing, Lestrade," Johnson sighed. "Well, not nothing. This case is closed, Lestrade. Over."

Lestrade's neutral expression faltered. "Sir?"

"Trust me on this. You want to have a long, successful career at Scotland Yard? Let this one go." Lestrade looked down at his feet and took a long, slow breath. When he looked up, his eyes met and held the older inspector's gaze with eyes that seemed to suck the very light and warmth from the room. Johnson shivered, expecting – hell, he didn't know what he was expecting from the man, but Lestrade only uttered a single word.

"Why?"

Johnson stared at him. Was he serious? But Lestrade held his gaze, waiting for an answer. Johnson licked his lips. His voice, when he spoke, came out a whisper. "Children gone missing? Blonde, blue-eyed children? Turning up dead, overdosed on opium, with no other marks on their bodies? Only one thing that could be." When he realized Lestrade was still waiting, he cursed. "Slave traders, Lestrade. Slavers took them. Someone miscalculated the dosage needed to keep them asleep, or docile, or whatever."

Lestrade tilted his head slightly. "Then…," he stopped, uncertain. "We should go after them," he said resolutely, finding himself.

"Are you daft?" The words exploded from the older man's mouth before he was even aware they had formed in his mind. "Or mad?" Lestrade didn't understand. That much was obvious. The man had no idea what he was suggesting. "Do you really want to go up against a batch of slave traders?"

Lestrade blinked. For a moment he was completely thrown, and Johnson wanted to shake him. What did he think he was suggesting, then? A polite conversation where they asked them nicely to stop kidnapping children? When the younger man finally pulled himself together enough to answer, his words were slow, halting, and made Johnson's blood run cold.

"Isn't that our job?"

Johnson swore again. Shoving himself away from his desk, he stalked over to the window and stared unseeingly through the glass pane. Memories long buried came back, unbidden and unwanted, of a childhood spent hungry, cold, and afraid. Mostly afraid, especially after his older sister and, quite frankly, his staunchest protector, had disappeared in broad daylight, taken on the street by person or persons unknown, never to be seen again. Her body was never found, but then, neither were any of the others. A lot of children had disappeared that year.

Sometimes he wondered if their parents had sold her, or if someone had simply seen an opportunity and taken it. He knew she had not run away; at the very least she would have taken him with her. She hadn't been killed in some dark alley – again, there had been no body. And after she had disappeared his parents had kept a tight watch over him, as if terrified he might meet the same fate.

Taking a shaky breath, he turned back to look at the man standing in his office. Lestrade was young, yes. Incredibly naive, but apparently devoted to his duty. Good in a fight and willing to follow orders. He had showed initiative and demonstrated a good head for investigation. If the first two did not get him killed, he would make a great inspector one day, provided this place allowed it.

Johnson took another breath, and felt a stab of panic in his chest, one that was almost immediately quelled by an almost ominous sense of calm. Lestrade was still watching him with impossibly wide eyes. Still waiting for an answer, and with a sudden clarity the older inspector realized that *this* was the moment that would make or break the man before him, and which depended entirely upon him.

"Damn it!"

Johnson sighed. Scowling, he moved away from the window. Closing the gap between the two of them and standing way closer than either man was comfortable with, he met Lestrade's gaze and held it.

"If you want to do this, Lestrade, really want to, then you'd better be ready for the consequences."

The door swung open with a bang, and both men started. Johnson swore as Adams looked from one man to the other.

"What the hell are you two doing?" He shook his head. "Never mind, I don't want to know. Come on, I need your help."

"With what?" Johnson was already following him out of the office. He motioned for Lestrade to follow.

"Moving a body." Johnson felt rather than saw Lestrade stop in his tracks. When neither of the older inspectors responded, he started up again, quickening his pace to catch back up. Once he had done so, Adams explained, keeping his voice low all the while. "Smith must have done something stupid again, because he's unconscious in the back alley and by the looks of it, I'd say he took a quite a beating."

Johnson closed his eyes briefly. "He swears he doesn't do it on purpose."

"Maybe, but he also doesn't *not* do it on purpose." Adams growled as they stepped out the back entrance of the building and into the alleyway. At least Lestrade seemed to know to keep his mouth shut.

Smith was lying face down in the street with a puddle of blood beneath him, and for all of a heartbeat Johnson was sure he was dead. Then Adams bent down to feel for a pulse and the man flinched and let out a moan.

"Idiot," Adams spat. "Help me turn him over."

They got the inspector on his back, and Johnson winced at the man's bloodied face. "What the hell did you get yourself into this time, John?"

"No broken bones, no signs of bleeding," Adams reported. "Other than the obvious. Lestrade, you want his feet or an arm?"

Lestrade stood halfway out the door, not exactly staring. "Feet," he offered without missing a beat.

"You sure?" Johnson asked.

Lestrade rolled his shoulders. "You two are more evenly matched in height. It will be easier if you two each get an arm."

He was right. Johnson grabbed one arm while Adams took the other. More than that, Lestrade was calm and collected even though he had no idea what the hell was going on. The three of them lifted Smith and began the arduous task of moving him inside.

The man's weight was easier to manage with three, but it was still awkward trying to get him around corners and through doors. All three inspectors were out of breath by the time they had succeeded in manhandling their fallen comrade through the door to his office.

"Put him on the floor," Adams grunted. Smith was still out and landed perhaps a bit harder than anyone intended, but he was also heavy. Straightening up, Johnson grimaced as his body reminded him that he had been in a bar fight all of three days ago. He was not the only one reminded, if the way Lestrade was rolling his shoulder was any indication. The movement caught Adams' attention.

"You going to ask what happened?" he demanded, glaring at the younger man. Lestrade looked back at him, eyes shuttered, expression neutral.

"Sir?"

Adams swore and turned away. Lestrade turned his attention back to the unconscious man.

"He'll be all right." Johnson hoped he would, anyway. Smith had a knack for accidentally stumbling into cases that got him in trouble, primarily with other inspectors at Scotland Yard. Johnson supposed that he should be grateful that Lestrade had at least not ended up partnered with Smith. That would have been an absolute disaster.

Johnson remembered what he had agreed to in his office earlier and reconsidered. "This is what happens when you ask the wrong questions about the wrong people." He hoped Lestrade would take the hint.

The younger man looked up, and for a moment Johnson was sure he would not. Then something clicked in those dark eyes. Lestrade swallowed, and nodded. Adams looked back in time to see and immediately started swearing again.

"You lot are going to be the death of me," he snarled when he finally regained control of himself.

When Smith came to an hour later, Adams insisted on taking him home. "And whatever you two are up to, I don't want to hear it. Don't get yourselves killed until I get back."

Johnson shrugged and turned back to Lestrade. "You heard the man." He smiled against the sudden panic threatening to claw its way out of his chest. Lestrade's eyebrows narrowed as if he didn't get the joke. "Since apparently Smith's current condition has done nothing to make you reconsider, where do we start?"

"Talk to the doctor again. Get a more complete report on the other victims. See if there have been any others farther back. Maybe give missing persons another look." Lestrade was rapidly becoming an entirely different person when he was working a case. Johnson was not certain the man was entirely aware of the change.

"Then what?"

Lestrade shrugged.

"What if you don't come up with anything?"

No reply. Johnson rubbed his face with his hand. God help him, he was going to do it. "Make a list of potential cover-ups. Businesses that might be fronts."

Lestrade blinked. "I don't know any…"

"I do," Johnson cut him off. "I can think of a few that wouldn't be above something like this. Can I trust you to go to the morgue while I start working on the lists?

Lestrade hesitated, then nodded.

"And it goes without saying you shouldn't talk about this to anyone." Another nod. "Good. If you aren't back in three hours I'm going to assume you got yourself murdered."

"Yes, sir," Lestrade started out the door before pausing and turning to look back at the older man. "Sir?"

"What?"

Lestrade wavered, then decided to press on. "Why are you doing this?"

Johnson sat heavily at his desk, refusing to meet the man's eyes as he did so. "Because I haven't thought about Cynthia in years," that remark really didn't explain anything. Forcing himself to look up, he added, "And because you're right. It is our job."

From the unexpected sympathy he suddenly read in the younger inspector's eyes, maybe he understood more of that explanation than Johnson would have thought.

Lestrade managed to make his way back to the morgue without incident. He even managed to find the doctor from the previous day, a Doctor Marcus Holdsworth.

"Ah, good morning, Inspector, Lestrade, was it?" Holdsworth had beady eyes that darted back and forth when he talked, but he was at least talking. He offered a smile that seemed genuine enough and offered his hand.

"Yes, Doctor, good morning," Lestrade took the proffered hand in a brief handshake. "Thank you again for your assistance yesterday."

"Of course, of course! Always happy to help." Holdsworth grew somber. "I can't say I'm pleased to have identified the boy and located his family, it's far too much of a tragedy when something like this happens, but it's far more often that we end up with nothing." Lestrade nodded in understanding, and the doctor collected himself. "That being said, I doubt you came around a second time just to say thank you."

Lestrade tilted his head in acknowledgment. "I was actually hoping to ask you about the other children you mentioned. Maybe I can match them to some of our missing persons' files."

Holdsworth nodded. "I have the reports in my office, if you'd care to accompany me, Inspector."

Lestrade followed him to his office. Inside, the desk was shiny mahogany, the chair behind it leather and plainly built for comfort. Sleek bookshelves lined one wall and matched the desk, and a dark blue rug complimented the dark wooden floor. The effect would have been luxuriant, had there not also been files and loose papers stacked on nearly every available surface. How the man could find, let alone keep track of, anything in his office was beyond the inspector.

Holdsworth sat down at his desk and promptly disappeared behind a mountain of files. His disembodied voice floated through the mess while Lestrade remained near the door, unwilling to risk disturbing the barely controlled chaos before him. "I set the relevant files aside, just in case. I have to admit I was hoping you'd be back, Inspector."

Lestrade simply waited while the other man searched. Idle conversation had never been a strength of his, and past attempts had been awkward at best, and usually painful. His sister seemed to be the one exception – he had never had much difficulty in expressing himself to her, and on the few occasions he found himself at a loss for words, she usually understood him anyway.

Holdsworth continued talking as he poked through various drawers. "You start to get used to it, after a while, Inspector, and I suppose that's a terrible thing to admit, but maybe it's a way for the mind to protect itself, to learn not to let these things get to you after a while." He shook his head as he continued. "Never did get used to dealing with the little ones, though...," he sighed. "Here it is!"

Holdsworth straightened and offered Lestrade the files. "I'll let you alone to look through those, here's probably not the best place, but there's a meeting room down the hall.

You're more than welcome to set up in, and I'll be downstairs if you have any questions."

"Thank you, Doctor," Lestrade excused himself. He found the meeting room with little difficulty and settled down to work.

Johnson checked his watch again. Lestrade had been gone for three hours and fifteen minutes now, and while he did not think they had gotten far enough on this investigation yet for the man to have gotten himself killed, something had to be holding him up. So far the rookie had been consistently early for work, and that coupled with his precise demeanor had led Johnson to believe that Lestrade was not the sort of man to lose track of time. Johnson had all but told him to be back in three hours, and Lestrade had seemed to understand that.

And while fifteen minutes was not terribly late, in this case, Johnson was beginning to worry. It was a dangerous city even without deciding to investigate slave traders, and for experienced inspectors as well. Lestrade had been promoted to this position all of three days ago.

Twenty minutes late.

He was going to have to go looking for the man. Standing up, Johnson considered the lists he had put together while the other inspector was out. It was not the sort of information one just left lying around. He picked up the two sheets of paper and folded them carefully in half, and then again. Folding them once more he tucked them into his own notebook, where the only way someone might come across them was after removing them from his corpse, and if that were the case, it would no longer matter who saw what he had written.

The door opened as Johnson pushed in his chair, and Lestrade entered the office. Johnson scowled at him. "What happened to three hours?" He demanded.

Lestrade looked at him. "Sorry, sir," he apologized, "it took longer than I thought it would to copy the information from the files." He looked around the office restlessly. "Five of them in the last three months, sir, not including the Abbott boy."

Johnson pulled the chair back out from his desk and sat down. "All the same?"

"Yes, sir,"

Johnson frowned. Rubbing his forehead, he asked, "Opium?"

"Yes, sir,"

"Still planning to check those against the missing persons' files?" Johnson didn't hold out much hope there, but he supposed it never hurt to be certain.

Lestrade nodded.

"You took notes on the doctor's files, are they in that shorthand of yours?" Another nod. "Copy those out for me. Be careful though, the less attention we attract, and the fewer questions we have to answer, the better." Johnson drummed his fingers against his desk. "I threw a couple of lists together, but I think for now it's better if I hold on to them." Lestrade did not argue, though Johnson thought he caught a flash of impatience in the younger man's eyes.

"We want to be careful, Lestrade. We need to take things slowly, make certain of every step. No sense getting killed because we rushed into something." Johnson paused, then added, "And other cases are probably going to come up. We can't ignore those just to go chasing after a bunch of traders. You understand?"

"Yes, sir," Lestrade agreed dutifully, then added, "I'd like to check missing persons first. I can start copying my notes for you as soon as I've finished, as long as nothing else comes up."

Johnson nodded, and Lestrade excused himself.

Nothing came up. Lestrade went through the missing person files with painstaking care only to find absolutely nothing relevant to the case. Once he finished, he returned to Johnson's office. The older Inspector had found an extra chair in Lestrade's absence, and cleared off a corner of his desk as well. He nodded Lestrade to the chair as the man came in.

"Any luck?" he asked, as Lestrade took a seat and started copying his notes. The other inspector frowned and shook his head. Johnson almost felt a twinge of sympathy but quashed it down. Lestrade had to learn how things worked here at the Yard, since he apparently somehow hadn't quite managed it yet. "It was a long shot, Lestrade."

The inspector only nodded and kept writing.

It took him the rest of the shift to finish copying out his notes. When he did he simply offered them to Johnson without flourish.

Johnson slipped them into his notebook for later consideration. He was not about to leave anything incriminating lying around in his office. Standing and allowing himself to stretch slightly, he looked at the other inspector. "It can wait for tomorrow," he told the young man. "I'll walk you out, Lestrade."

Johnson watched him visibly resist the urge to argue. They left the office. Johnson locked the door behind him, for all the good it would do.

They left the Yard without incident, and parted ways on the street. "Don't get killed before I see you again." Johnson grumbled halfheartedly after the other inspector.

Lestrade continued down the street. His eyes darted about in an attempt to see everything at once; he had still not gotten completely used to the city even after all this time. Getting clipped by a cab even once was still one time too many, and an experience the man had no intention of ever repeating.

It was not until he crossed the threshold of the flat he shared with his sister and closed the door behind him that he was able to relax. Allowing himself a deep sigh, Lestrade removed his hat and ran a hand absently through his hair as he tried to think about anything other than six dead children, dutifully and impersonally laid out in his notebook.

"Is that you, Giles?" The opportunity for a not entirely unwelcome distraction presented itself in the form of his sister calling from the kitchen. "Had enough yet? You could always go back to Fleet Street."

Lestrade stifled a second sigh and made his way to the back room. "You could always go back to the manor," he retorted, and was rewarded with a guffaw of laughter that would never be deemed proper for a lady, but seemed to fit Kristina perfectly.

"Then who would look after you, I wonder." It was not a question; Kristina was thoroughly convinced that her brother not only needed constant looking after, but would scarcely last a week if something were to happen to her and he were left to his own devices.

She greeted him with a smile and brandished a spoon at him. "Enough fretting. Whatever is on your mind will still be there tomorrow. Right now dinner's ready."

Lestrade obligingly sat down at the table. Kristina joined him, and insisted on serving him even as he raised an eyebrow at her. "I can get my own food," he pointed out mildly. Kristina snorted.

"The Mullenses next door got a kitten. Poor creature is so small, I'm pretty sure the mice are going to be chasing him, not the other way around," she said conversationally, and Lestrade tried to remember which set of neighbors she meant. "They have the babe that cries through the night, Giles. And the boys are so skinny they look like a brisk gust of wind could snap them clean in half."

Lestrade remained silent, preferring to focus on his meal, but that never made any difference when Kristina was involved. She kept right on talking as if he had spoken. It was, most of the time, a relief to be around someone who knew him so well.

Kristina shook her head. "I only hope the cat works. These mice are a pestilence, and that's for certain!" She stabbed at her potato viciously and immediately changed the subject. "So are they giving you a hard time, or did something happen? I haven't seen you this worked up in a long time."

She sized her brother up critically. "I have a hard time believing someone could have gotten under your skin in only three days," she decided after a moment's consideration. Lestrade met her gaze to find his own dark eyes staring back at him thoughtfully.

"I don't think I should talk about it," he admitted, finally. "It's…," he hesitated, trying to find the right words. Kristina waited.

Lestrade studied his fork for a long moment before continuing. "I think I was supposed to ignore something," he admitted. "And now that I haven't, I may have put myself and another inspector in a dangerous situation." It wasn't anything near what he wanted to say, but he had no idea what that even was.

Kristina pressed her lips together. "I'm sure he can take care of himself," she pointed out. "You, on the other hand..."

"I can take care of myself," Lestrade snapped, catching himself too late. He met his sister's gaze defiantly.

Kristina sighed. "I'm sure you can, Giles," she conceded. She had to hope that he knew his job well enough to stay alive. "No need to go out looking for trouble to prove it, all right?"

Lestrade did not comment. They both knew trouble came looking for him more often than not.

They finished their meal in a not entirely comfortable silence. Afterward they cleared the table, washed the dinner dishes, and tidied up the kitchen. The after-dinner cleanup complete, Kristina settled down with a sewing kit and the ill-fated jacket from Lestrade's first day as an inspector to see if it could be salvaged; Lestrade found himself going through his notebook note by note in case there was something – anything – he had missed. He continued doggedly poring through it long after his sister gave up on trying to get his attention and left the neatly mended jacket spread out on the table – the slit in it now held together with stitches so small as to be invisible under all but the most discerning eye – on her way to bed.

Four

The following morning Lestrade again made it to Inspector Johnson's office before said inspector arrived. This time there were no files to sort, no paperwork of any kind in need of organizing. Nor did Lestrade have any other sort of direction on what to do until the man *did* arrive, other than not to get himself killed.

Lestrade was not an idiot. He had a very specific and well thought out reason for almost everything he did, with the exception of a few habits picked up in his youth that he had never quite been able to shake.

He would never be counted among the most intelligent of men, perhaps, and even his own sister had often despaired of his ability when it came to his somewhat limited education, but Lestrade had found that more often than not hard work and stubbornness would get the job done just as well as natural ability, even if it took a little longer.

Neither daft nor mad, the young inspector forced himself to sit in the chair that had been relegated to him the previous day and wait for the other man. Giving in to the need to be doing something, he took out his notebook and started on it again.

Lestrade had stopped counting how many times he had been through the thing.

"Lestrade!" The inspector's head jerked up and around to find Adams standing impatiently in the open doorway. "I don't know what you've got in that notebook that's so fascinating that you didn't hear me the first three times, but around here a man doesn't last long if he isn't constantly aware of his surroundings."

Lestrade stood, tucking his notebook safely away in his jacket in the same fluid motion. "Sorry, sir." He ducked his head almost nervously.

Adams had neither the patience nor the time for dithering, polite or otherwise. "Never mind. You'll learn. Or not. You spent a lot of time over on Fleet Street as a constable?"

"Yes, sir."

"Good. Come on. I need a familiar eye for the territory – and a familiar face for the regulars." He turned and was halfway down the hall before he realized the younger inspector had not followed. Turning back, he glowered at the smaller man. "Something wrong with your hearing, lad?"

Lestrade stared up at him but held his ground. "No sir," he conceded, his expression giving away nothing.

Adams felt his eyebrows inch toward his hairline. "Then why, Inspector Lestrade, are you still standing here instead of following me over to Fleet Street like an obedient, freshly promoted inspector should?"

Lestrade's lips pursed slightly as he considered the question. "Inspector Johnson said not to get killed before he sees me again," he said.

Adams snorted in spite of himself. "Leave him a note telling him where and why you've gone. If he has a problem, when you come back you face him like a man."

Lestrade did not quite frown, but pulled his notebook back out of its inner jacket pocket. Tearing a sheet out, the man took far longer than Adams would have liked to write out a note with painstaking care. He settled it neatly on Johnson's desk, careful not to disturb anything. His task completed, he turned back to Adams expectantly.

Adams sighed. "Ready?" This time the rookie followed him from the room, through the building, and out onto the street.

There were too many constables standing around doing nothing. Too many bystanders as well. Adams opened his mouth to tell Lestrade to start dispersing their audience and quickly shut it again as the man elbowed one of the constables, a man nearly a head taller than the new inspector and twice as wide in the shoulders. Adams quickly reconsidered his plan of action and crossed his arms across his chest, content for the moment to watch.

"Watch it, you little... " the constable must have recognized Lestrade, because instead of finishing, he grinned. "Come to slum around with your old pals have you, laddie?"

Lestrade rolled his eyes. "Inspector now, Gregory," he reminded the man without animosity. "See what you and some of the others can do about our gawkers?" Phrased as a question, it was nothing less than an order. To the credit of both men, Constable Gregory offered a chipper if not entirely respectful salute and started making his rounds.

Adams watched as Lestrade watched the bigger man go, waiting to see whether or not he would need to step in. A moment passed, and Adams had begun to scan the area to see if anyone were actually in charge of the scene when out of the corner of his eye he saw Lestrade whip his body around to stare at a group of constables.

"Somebody get Collins away from the body!" he snapped, his eyes wide in alarm. He followed the man's gaze to see two red-faced constables escorting a third discreetly away from the body and out of sight down a side alley. Those policemen remaining looked either mildly amused or more than slightly abashed, the latter steadfastly refusing to look in Lestrade's direction in an attempt to avoid meeting his gaze.

Gregory returned. "Anything else?" he asked, and Lestrade seemed to remember himself. Turning to meet Adams' gaze with more caution than was currently warranted, the younger inspector made his deference clear without so much as uttering a word.

Adams waved his hand at the man. "Go on, Lestrade. What now?"

Lestrade considered the scene. "We don't need this many constables milling around, Gregory. Did anyone here actually see what happened?"

Gregory winced. "Collins did. I think Andrews got here just after – might be worth talking to." Lestrade nodded.

"Send the rest of them on their way unless they have anything useful to offer?" He was scanning the area as he spoke.

"Sure thing, Lestrade." If the man noticed that Gregory had left, he gave no indication. He also seemed unaware when Adams sidled up next to him, though to his credit he did not startle when the older inspector spoke.

"You have every right to insist they use your title, or at least offer some token of respect," he pointed out, his voice low. "What will you do when you find yourself facing off with one of them because he didn't like the orders you gave?"

Lestrade's eyes continued scanning as he answered, his own voice equally soft. "I don't need to, not with Gregory. And the others will follow his lead even if they don't care for me."

"And if Gregory disagrees with you?" Adams pressed. Lestrade did not answer, instead throwing up his hand in a "come here" gesture. He had found his intended target.

"Andrews!" A skinny, freckle-faced young man looked up and made a beeline for the two Inspectors.

"Sir?" He stopped short in front of them. "Inspectors?" He corrected himself, then his eyes widened in surprise. "Lestrade? Er, Inspector Lestrade, sir? What can I do for you, sir?"

Adams found it interesting that Lestrade waved the man's attempts off. "What happened?"

Andrews straightened. "It was already over when I got here, sir – Lestrade," he admitted, but continued anyway. "The body – the woman, was lying on the sidewalk there. The window was broken. Collins was staring at her, you know how he is about blood and corpses, Lestrade – sir. Anyway, people started gathering, and you know how it is, and…" The constable must have read something in Lestrade's expression that Adams did not, because he abruptly stopped talking.

Lestrade took a deep breath. "At what time did you arrive, Andrews?" he asked, reaching for his notebook.

"Oh, it was about eight-fifteen, sir," Andrews replied vaguely. Lestrade raised an eyebrow, and the constable winced. "I didn't check the time. But I was down by the tailor's when I heard someone scream, and that was at eight-fifteen, certainly. I'm not sure how long it took me to get from there to here, and I should have checked, Lestrade, but I didn't."

Lestrade made a note in his notebook before asking, "Did you see anyone in the window?"

"No, sir."

"Did anyone leave the building after the incident?"

"No,"

"Did anyone recognize the body? Anyone approach saying they knew her?"

Andrews shook his head. "No, sir. Plenty of people gathered to stare, but no one spoke up saying they knew her."

Lestrade looked up from his notebook and considered the man standing before him. "Can you tell us anything at all that might help?"

Andrews slouched miserably and shook his head. "No, sir."

Lestrade waved him off without another word. Andrews left gratefully, trotting off in Gregory's direction. Lestrade took a deep breath and looked around for Collins. Another wave brought the still queasy constable over.

"Lestrade. Inspector, I mean." Collins greeted him tersely. "Congratulations."

Lestrade ignored the small talk. "Forget to breathe through your mouth?" he asked pointedly.

"Gregory says it makes me look like a fish out of water, mouth all agape," Collins admitted sheepishly. "I already don't look particularly bright." Changing back to the reason for the inspectors' visit, he continued. "I was on the corner there when I heard the glass break. Turned in time to see her hit the ground. She fell from the second story – by the time I looked up there wasn't anyone else in sight. Nobody came out of the house either, unless they did it after I stepped away just now."

"Or while you were trying not to vomit on the body?" Lestrade asked dryly. Collins winced.

"It's not just the smell, Lestrade. That copper tang in the air. Seeing her like that – I know I should be used to it by now..." he trailed off uncomfortably. Lestrade offered no reassurance.

"What time?"

"It was ten after eight when she fell. Parker got here almost immediately; I sent him to check to see if anybody was home, but he never reported back, at least not to me." Collins swallowed rapidly, still trying to regain control of his stomach.

"Anything you can tell me about the state of the woman?" Lestrade asked, and the other man's face took on a greenish cast.

"I'm sorry, Lestrade." Collins shook his head. "I thought it was getting better…"

Lestrade looked around. "See if you can find Parker anywhere. If you can't, go check the house. See if anyone was home – if anyone still is. Try to find out who she was and how she was related to anyone in the household."

"Yes, sir," Collins looked relieved not to be going back to the corpse. Adams wondered whether Lestrade was going to get to that part himself. So far the man had done well to try to restore some order and get some idea of what had happened, but sooner or later he was going to have to approach the dead woman.

Almost as if he had read the older inspector's mind, Lestrade turned his attention to the reason for their presence. Approaching with care, his eyes scanning the area around and above them for anything that might be important, Lestrade stopped at the body of the dead woman and knelt carefully beside her for a better look.

The woman had fallen backwards through the window: she had landed face up with her feet toward the building. It was obvious from the pooling blood that she had hit her head; less obvious were what other injuries she might have sustained. Broken glass lay around and, most likely, under her.

Gregory joined them by the corpse. "Parker's useless. Never even made it to the front step. God only knows where he's gotten to. I sent Collins home before he embarrassed himself, Lestrade. You expect too much of the boy."

Lestrade shrugged.

"Anyway," Gregory continued, "only person in the house was this thin slip of a maid, hidden in the pantry and sobbing. Says the house belongs to a Mr. Aaron Childers. He and the deceased – a Miss Millicent Rose – were engaged. The maid heard them arguing but thought nothing of it; apparently, they argued a lot. She heard something break and thought Mr. Childers had lost his temper again. She hid in the pantry until she heard him leave, then went to see what the mess had been. When she saw the broken window, she looked down and saw Miss Rose on the pavement. Went and hid back in the pantry." Gregory looked uncomfortable.

"Poor thing seemed to think I was either going to beat her senseless or drag her off to prison."

"Any idea where Mr. Childers went?" Lestrade asked. Gregory shook his head.

"I'll leave Andrews here to wait for him to come back." The constable offered. "Give him a chance to redeem himself. Should he bring him down to the Yard or keep him here?"

Lestrade hesitated, and Adams stepped in. "Tell him we're investigating the murder of his fiancée and would like him to stop by Scotland Yard at his earliest convenience to ask some questions. Make it clear that by that we mean immediately. He can ask for Inspector Adams at the front desk." Adams offered the constable a humorless grin. "If he tries to run, bring him in."

Gregory's eyes flickered to Lestrade for the briefest of moments. "Yes, sir. Anything else I can do for you?"

Adams considered the man. "Stay and see to the crime scene. Someone should be here for the body shortly. Come on, Lestrade. That's enough fresh air for one day."

Lestrade's brows furrowed. "Sir?" Beside him, Gregory nearly snorted. His expression smoothed out at the last second, leaving nothing to suggest amusement at the new inspector's expense.

Lestrade ignored the constable, and Adams tried not to sigh. "Never mind, Lestrade."

"Where the hell have you been?" Johnson was livid when Lestrade finally showed up; he had spent the last several hours imagining the rookie inspector dead in a ditch somewhere after asking the wrong person the wrong question.

Johnson had arrived that morning to find his office surprisingly empty, the young man nowhere to be seen. Smith had not seen him that morning, and nobody else would have cared enough to notice. Johnson's first thought had immediately been that the lad had gotten himself in trouble; halfway out the door he reconsidered and allowed that even the usually early Lestrade might simply be running late for once.

The man was not an imbecile; Johnson had gotten enough of his measure by now that he was certain that any youthful impatience would not be enough to outweigh the warnings he had received about going off on his own. More than that, Lestrade seemed to keep his own counsel unless pressed, and that made it highly unlikely that the man had talked to the wrong person even unintentionally.

As the minutes ticked away and became hours, Johnson began to reconsider. It was obvious that Lestrade felt strongly about the case, strongly enough to ignore Johnson's most fervent warnings to leave it alone. It was equally clear that while Lestrade seemed to defer to Johnson while he was present, the man had no compunction about acting independently when he saw fit. He had done so with the little boy's mother on his second day as inspector, and he would likely do it again if he felt the need. It was a trait that could serve him well – or get him killed.

Smith tried to reassure him by pointing out that so far no body had turned up, and if Lestrade had gotten himself killed for asking stupid questions his body would most certainly turn up somewhere as a warning to anyone who might have been stupid enough to encourage such questions.

"What kind of questions could he be asking to get him in that kind of trouble in his first week anyway?" Smith asked lightheartedly. Seeing the other man's expression darken, he grew somber. "What have you two gotten yourselves into?" he asked, his voice low.

Johnson shook his head instead of answering. "Never mind, John," he said. "You've enough to worry about as it is."

Smith shrugged. "All right, then. Let me know if you get into trouble." With that, he was gone.

Johnson was just about to grab Smith and go looking for the erstwhile inspector anyway when Lestrade himself turned up. A quick glance revealed that the man was both very much alive and significantly undamaged, and Johnson lost it.

"What the hell is wrong with you? What makes you think that it's even remotely all right to go off on your own? To go off without telling anyone? You could have been killed! And whose fault do you think it is if you end up in a ditch somewhere? Mine! It'll be my fault for encouraging this nonsense instead of shutting you down right from the start like I should have! What in god's name were you doing running around London when you should have been here?"

Johnson paused to catch his breath, ready to start again because apparently what the young man needed was a reminder that he was the newcomer here and Johnson was the one in charge of making the decisions and that it was in no way acceptable to go off on his own whenever he felt like it.

"Sorry, sir." The words came out nearly a whisper. Lestrade was, for the first time since Johnson had met him, refusing to meet his eyes. Staring resolutely at the ground, every muscle rigid, his face nearly white rather than the expected red, the younger inspector seemed to be only just holding himself in place instead of darting for the still open doorway.

Johnson considered the man before him carefully. "Lestrade." He managed to even out his tone, but the Inspector still flinched. Johnson forced back a sigh and tried again. "Where were you, Inspector?"

Adams chose exactly that moment to appear in the doorway. Inviting himself in, he came to lean against the wall next to Johnson's desk. "He was with me," he offered, his voice low, his expression accusatory. "We left you a note. Now what the devil are you to up to that's got you so worked up that you could be heard clear down the hall?"

Johnson shrugged noncommittally or tried to, and Adams rolled his eyes. Turning to Lestrade, who had not dared to so much as twitch since the other inspector's arrival, he barked an order.

"Tea. Now. Three cups, Lestrade."

Lestrade recovered enough to manage a strangled "Yes, sir," and excused himself. Adams closed the door behind him, turning the lock before rejoining the other inspector.

"What was that about?" he asked calmly. Johnson sighed and ran a hand through his hair.

"I wasn't trying to terrify him," he admitted, somewhat sheepishly. "I just wanted to get the point across."

"Well, I'm pretty sure you succeeded on both counts," Adams said dryly. "But that's not what I meant. He's been here less than a week. Even Smith took about two months before he started getting into trouble. Lestrade cannot possibly have gotten into anything on his own to have you this worried already, which means it has to be a group effort. Now what are you two doing?"

Johnson felt his mouth go dry, and wondered exactly how far he could trust the man standing in front of him.

He had known the man as an inspector for four years. Longer as a constable. He had a good head on his shoulders: considered his words and actions carefully, remained calm in a crisis, and was not easily intimidated. He also had a knack for staying out of trouble. He kept his head down, his mouth closed. Didn't ask questions. He came and went with ease, and in spite of his apparent soft spot for Inspector Smith (friendship was, possibly, too strong a word) could work with just about anybody at Scotland Yard without getting himself into trouble.

As far as Johnson knew, the other man was not involved in anything illegal himself. Nor did he get involved with others who were – the man simply seemed content to keep to himself and mind his own business.

Johnson had no idea what any of that meant in the face of what he and Lestrade were now trying to do. He had no idea how the other man would react. Would he think they were idiots for getting involved? Would he turn them over to someone who might take issue with their interference? Would he simply turn around and leave, ignoring the two for his own safety? Johnson had absolutely no way of knowing, even after all these years.

He was fairly certain that Adams would not help them.

"It's nothing," Johnson said, and Adams bit back a laugh that was more bitter than anything else.

"Of course it's nothing," he said, disbelief evident in every word. The man suddenly looked worn, for all that he was the younger of the two of them. "You're going to get that boy killed," he warned.

By the time Lestrade returned with three cups of tea that were far too strong and not nearly sweet enough, a tentative silence had settled between the two men. Lestrade himself was still a shade too pale, but at least his hands were steady as he offered first Johnson, then Adams battered cups.

He retreated to a corner of the room automatically and busied himself with his tea.

Johnson took a sip and grimaced, setting the cup aside. Adams drank his silently and left without another word.

Lestrade was jumpy for the rest of the day. Johnson was convinced the other inspector was watching him out of the corner of his eye as if expecting some sort of attack, but since it was nothing overt, and he certainly had no proof other than a strong feeling, he let the matter go rather than risk doing more damage.

Lestrade's earlier reaction concerned him. Whether it had been a response to the older inspector's anger or simply to criticism, neither boded well for the man's future at Scotland Yard. Their superiors, their fellow inspectors, even the people they were allegedly there to protect could be expected to take issue with him at some point, and Lestrade needed to be able to deal with that. Lestrade had to be able to stand his ground here if he were going to survive.

Perhaps more worrying, and for reasons that Johnson did not quite understand, Lestrade's reaction earlier had been completely at odds with everything the other Inspector knew of the man so far. He had held his own in a tavern brawl on his first day and battled his way through a terror of hospitals on his second. He had steadfastly refused to walk away from what he perceived as his duty every time the chance came to do so, even when it would have been safer. It was not, from what Johnson had seen this far, in Lestrade's nature to back down from a challenge.

Lestrade nearly caught the other inspector staring; his eyes darted away from Johnson's gaze and skittered about the room almost frantically before settling on the notebook he must have read through at least a dozen times already. Johnson frowned at this sudden attempt to…

To do what? To avoid conflict? To keep from angering the other inspector again? That hadn't seemed to matter before, not when a mother had been looking for her lost boy, and not when that boy turned out to have been one of several taken by slavers.

But Lestrade had been carefully, intentionally, and completely non-confrontational up until those moments. Yes, sir; no, sir; sorry, sir. Lestrade's speech was polite and precise, if unpolished, right up until a switch inside flipped and then those unnaturally dark eyes of his threatened to burn up anyone caught too long in their gaze. Then he didn't seem to care who he offended.

It was almost as if the man were two separate people. Johnson's frown deepened as he recalled Adams' claim that the well-mannered inspector was just an act, and he wondered if the man were right.

Who was the real Lestrade? And why did he feel the need to hide behind an almost infuriatingly polite mask?

Johnson sighed. They only thing either inspector was succeeding in doing was making the other more uncomfortable.

Five

"I need Lestrade."

It was almost a relief when Adams returned several hours later, demanding to borrow the rookie inspector. Johnson and Lestrade had spent both the remainder of the morning and the early part of the afternoon in an unproductive and increasingly frustrating attempt at sorting through Lestrade's notes on the slave trader case and trying to figure out not only what to do next, but how to do it without getting themselves killed as well.

Lestrade looked in dire need of escape, so Johnson simply waved him off and kept working.

"That constable came in. The big one you were chummy with earlier. Brought Mr. Childers in for questioning. Apparently he tried to run when they told him we had some questions," Adams explained as Lestrade followed him out of Johnson's office and down the hall. "Thought you might like to sit in, since you were there this morning."

"Thank you, sir," Lestrade replied. His expression was a poor imitation of its usual polite mask and his tone was somewhat terse. Whatever had happened earlier, the boy had not fully recovered himself.

Mr. Childers was waiting impatiently in what passed for their interrogation room, one of the men from Fleet Street standing close enough to discourage any more thoughts of escape.

"Constable," Adams nodded, and the lad returned the acknowledgment. Behind him Lestrade offered a muted greeting that caused the other man's eyebrows to briefly disappear under his helmet. Adams wondered if the young man knew something was off with the new inspector, but doubted he would get the opportunity to ask – or that the constable would answer honestly.

There seemed to be something between the two men. Not a friendship, precisely – friendships in their line of work were few and far between – but an understanding, and a sense of camaraderie. These two men knew each other well enough to trust each other – to a point.

Little as it was, it was more than most Yarders had these days, and it was enough that the constable would not willingly go around talking about Lestrade behind his back.

Adams turned his attention to the task at hand. Mr. Childers was still seated, glaring up at the newcomers resentfully as he waited to be questioned. This time, Adams took the lead.

"Mr. Aaron Childers, I presume?" He offered the man a polite smile that rivaled any Lestrade had given since his arrival at Scotland Yard. At the man's nod, Adams continued. "My condolences for your loss, Mr. Childers, and my most sincere apologies for any trouble we may have put you through, asking you to come down like this."

Childers shifted, and some of the bluster dissolved. Adams grinned inwardly and offered the constable the briefest of glances. "Outside," he ordered. As Gregory obeyed Adams turned his attention to Lestrade. "Over there. Take notes." Offering Childers a fake smile, he explained as Lestrade wordlessly retreated to a corner and found his notebook and pencil. "Lestrade here is new. Just got promoted a couple of days ago and is still learning the ropes."

Adams took a seat across from the man. "We just need to ask you a few questions, Mr. Childers, if that's all right."

"Of course," Childers had relaxed quite a bit by this time. "I'll tell you whatever I can."

"Thank you," Adams leaned forward and placed his hands on the table between them. "You were engaged to the deceased – a Miss Millicent Rose?" Childers nodded. "She had come to see you?"

"That morning," Childers replied somberly. "We had planned to spend the day together. A walk in the garden, an early lunch..." he trailed off and looked away, unwilling to allow either inspector to see the emotions playing across his face.

"There was an argument between you?" Childers turned sharply back to face Adams.

"Who told you that?" He forced himself to relax almost immediately. "The maid, I suppose. Nervous little thing." He looked at Lestrade, who stood dutifully taking notes, then back at Adams. "We did, yes. We often argued. Not over anything consequential." He frowned. "I have a bit of a temper, I'm afraid, and get worked up easily." He sighed.

"I'll admit, I threw a vase at the wall – I was that angry with her – but then I left. I never wanted to hurt her. I certainly did not want her dead. I loved her."

"Of course," Adams said agreeably, "You were engaged." He paused for a moment, considering. "Was anyone else in the house, other than the maid and the two of you?"

Childers shook his head. "I only employ the maid. She cooks and cleans, and I have little need for much else. And before you ask, no, I don't think she would have done it. I don't think she could have done it. The poor woman can't so much as kill a mouse when it gets into the kitchen. Another person is out of the question. And anyway, she and Millie – Miss Rose – got on rather well. She adored my fiancée."

"I see," Adams nodded in understanding. "Can you think of anyone who would have wanted to hurt your fiancée? Anyone?" He was interrupted as the door opened, and Inspector Flint stepped inside. Briskly he approached Adams and leaned over to whisper in the other inspector's ear.

"Suicide attempt. The woman killed herself." Adams resisted the urge to swear and turned to look up at Flint, who rested a hand comfortingly on his shoulder. "Superintendent's taken a special interest in this case, Inspector. He's taking over for you. Thanks you for everything you've done so far."

Adams swallowed back the bile that rose in his throat and stood. "I'll leave you to deliver the good news, then. Come on, Lestrade." He turned away from Childers and forced himself not to storm out the door, ignoring the sympathetic look Flint shot after him.

Flint wasn't bad, as far as crooked policemen went. He was smart – perhaps a bit too smart for his current position – but mostly harmless. Mischievous but never malicious, Adams suspected that in a more morally (and legally) upstanding Scotland Yard, Flint would have simply hovered quietly on the right side of the law rather than dabble in the criminal element as he did now. It was one of the reasons he and Adams usually managed to get along.

"Inspector? Inspectors?" Gregory was still waiting for them out in the hall. Adams ignored him and kept walking. Behind him constable and inspector exchanged a glance before following.

"Sir?" Lestrade ventured as they reached Adams' office and the inspector still had not offered an explanation. He stood, waiting cautiously for some sort of response, while Adams tried to regain some of his composure.

Finally he sighed, and looked from constable to inspector. "Close the door," he said, calmly enough. Far more calmly than he felt.

Gregory, who was closest, obliged. Only once the latch had clicked into place did Adams speak.

"The superintendent has taken a special interest in the case and will be seeing to it personally," he said, wishing the words tasted less bitter in his mouth.

Lestrade did not react, but Gregory frowned. "Sir? What does that mean?" the constable asked uncertainly.

"It means that Miss Rose is no longer our concern," Adams spat out. "It means that the case is closed. The official report will indicate that the woman killed herself."

He saw the doubt in the constable's eyes and – more tellingly – the sudden shuttering of Lestrade's. For a moment he wondered whether the younger members of the police force were all this naive, or whether he himself had simply grown jaded.

Gregory fought some inner battle quickly and came to a decision. "Yes, sir." He did not believe it, and he knew Adams did not either, but he also knew not to argue.

Lestrade remained unreadable, and suddenly Adams was certain that whatever it was that he and Johnson had gotten into, it was the new inspector's fault, and it was deadly serious.

Gregory elbowed Lestrade in a blatant display of insubordination, and the man's eyes blazed. Then his gaze dropped to the floor.

"Yes, sir," he echoed, his tone one of borderline rebellion.

Adams allowed himself to let out the breath he had been holding and retreated to the seat behind his desk, considering the two men before him all the while.

"Constable Gregory, was it?" He asked, willing some of the tension to settle. Years of practice kept his voice light and even.

"Yes, Inspector." Gregory looked as if he half expected to receive some sort of reprimand. Adams offered him a reassuring smile.

"And you've known our Inspector Lestrade how long?" He asked casually. No, the constable would not talk about the other man behind his back, but maybe, just maybe...

"Five years, sir. Since he came over from the River Police," Gregory replied cautiously.

"What's your impression of the man?" Adams leaned back in his chair and forced himself to relax. He wanted this to feel like a conversation, not an interrogation.

Gregory shrugged. "He gets the job done. Keeps to himself."

"Doesn't talk much," Adams offered. He received another shrug for his efforts.

"Not one for unnecessary chatter, that's true, sir." Gregory hesitated, considering how much to say. Behind him, Lestrade looked mildly uncomfortable with the conversation, but did not interject. "With respect, sir, most inspectors prefer constables that know how to keep their mouths closed and follow orders."

Adams did not bother to hide his amusement. "And would you say Lestrade knows how to do both of those things, Constable?" He asked. Gregory wavered, and Adams felt his good humor rapidly abandon him as the constable tried to find an acceptable response – one that would not betray the man currently standing in the room with him.

"He's a good man," Gregory finally settled on a different sort of answer, "even if sometimes he's a pain in the ass."

Adams laughed in spite of himself. "Go on, get out of here," he said, waving the man off. "And watch your back!" he called after him. Shaking his head, he turned his attention back to Lestrade.

"Well, now, Rookie, what are we going to do with you?" He asked aloud, though he certainly expected no answer from the man in front of him.

"Sir?" Lestrade asked, and Adams winced. He could feel a headache coming on.

"Close the door, Lestrade, and lock it. Then sit down. We need to talk."

Adams watched the young inspector cross the room and push the door closed, turning the lock before returning to sit on the other side of the desk. His expression was predictably bland, though there was an undercurrent of nervousness to his movements that the man could not quite hide.

For a moment Lestrade looked impossibly young and more than a little vulnerable, and Adams felt a sudden surge of sympathy for the other man. The feeling surprised him.

He leaned back in his chair to give Lestrade a little extra space. "So your reaction to Johnson reaming you out this morning. You wanna explain that?"

Lestrade froze in place, his shoulders hitched up around his ears, his eyes wide as Adams held his gaze and waited. Informal as the question had been, he fully expected an answer, and was willing to wait for as long as he had to.

Lestrade was silent for a long moment, then, "No, sir."

Adams felt his eyebrows raise. "What?"

Lestrade took a deep breath and answered, misery etched plainly across his face. "No, sir." He hesitated, then, "I don't want to explain it." He fell silent again, but Adams waited, sensing that the other inspector was not quite finished.

Finally Lestrade forced himself to speak, his voice so low Adams had to strain to hear it. "He surprised me. I wasn't expecting him to be so angry. And it reminded of something that happened a long time ago. It won't happen again, Inspector, you have my word on that. But I can't explain it any better than that."

"Can't? Or won't?" Adams challenged, but Lestrade did not look away. He did, however, seem to have pulled himself back together after some fashion.

Adams sighed. "Have it your, way, Lestrade, but it had better *not* happen again. You can't afford to let it. Not around here." He shook his head and rubbed his by-now throbbing temples. "What are you and Johnson up to?"

Lestrade's jaw tightened with a click, and Adams realized that the lad, at least, knew how to keep his mouth closed. The realization did not make him feel any better, as it only served as confirmation that something was going on between the two of them.

"I can already tell you're an idealistic young man," Adams told him wearily. "You probably joined the force to protect people or something like that. And maybe you've gotten this far and thought that you would be different, that you wouldn't ignore the things everyone else did. Or maybe you simply thought no one else really saw what was going on. And when you became an inspector, you were going to make things right. You were going to be different. Better."

Lestrade did not respond, but his eyes spoke far more than words would have. Adams had found the weakness in the man's façade, and it had done more than crack – it had shattered completely.

"So you saw something and couldn't ignore it," Adams continued. "And Johnson went along with it even though he knows better. And if you two are not very, very careful, you'll both end up dead in a gutter somewhere, and everything you've worked for so far will be for nothing."

Lestrade remained silent, but Adams could practically feel the anger radiating off the man.

Adams sighed. He was going to have to actually come out and say it.

"Damn it, Lestrade. Do you and Johnson really think you can take on the entire Scotland Yard by yourselves?" Lestrade blinked, and Adams resisted the urge to throw his hands in the air. "What do you think is going to happen? It doesn't matter what the initial case is, if you keep down this road, people are going to take notice. And then people are going to try to make you stop. People *here*, Lestrade. Inspectors. The superintendent. If you're going to insist on making enemies here, you're going to need people on your side as well if you want to survive. If you want anything to change."

Lestrade blinked again, and Adams realized he had completely surprised the younger inspector with his speech. Hell, he had surprised himself. Up until now his main goal had been to keep his head down, stay out of trouble, and try not to get killed. Whatever this was, it went against all three of those principles.

"Inspector Johnson says it's slave traders," Lestrade finally spoke, his voice low.

Adams swore. "You don't start small, do you?"

Six

Johnson looked up as Adams entered his office without knocking. He waited patiently as the inspector closed the door behind him and locked it before coming to sit down on the other side of the desk. When Adams leaned forward, Johnson obliged and mirrored the action.

"You're going to get that boy killed," Adams told him calmly, the glint in his eye betraying any attempt at sounding casual.

Johnson did not waver. "He'll do that on his own just fine," he told the other man. "I'm trying to keep him alive."

"By sending him after slave traders." Though he did not raise his voice, a muscle in Adams' jaw twitched furiously.

"Again, his idea."

Adams swore. "You're gonna fight slave traders? Why?" he demanded.

Johnson offered a wry grin. "Because it's our job," he told the other man. "Because Lestrade's right about that. And I've been burying my head in the sand for far too long, trying to tell myself that as long as I don't do anything to make it worse, then I'm still a good person. That I'm still a good policeman."

Adams sighed. Lestrade was right, and Johnson was right, and Adams was an idiot for getting involved.

"What do you have so far?" he asked, taking the other man completely by surprise.

Smith showed up in Johnson's office the next morning, eyes bright, his smirk barely contained. "I'm in."

"Pardon?" Johnson did not look up from his papers. He could still feel Smith rolling his eyes.

"Whatever it is, I'm in. Whatever you two are working on that's got you whispering behind closed doors and even managed to drag Adams in when you know he goes out of his way to stay out of trouble, I want to be a part of it."

"Fine," Johnson grumbled. "But not here. Not now."

"When?" Smith wanted to know.

Johnson resisted the urge to grind his teeth together. "The four of us conspiring together is sure to attract unwanted attention. So not here, not now. I don't know when or where. I'll let you know when I figure something out."

Lestrade spoke up from his corner of the desk. "My sister keeps asking if I've made any friends yet."

Both inspectors turned to stare at him. "What?"

Lestrade continued to stare at his notebook, though he was obviously not reading a word of it. A faint reddish tinge had crept into his normally sallow complexion. "My sister. She wants to know if I've made any new inspector friends."

It was the first time Johnson could remember the other man initiating a conversation on his own. It was the second time he had mentioned that he had a sister, or any family at all. Johnson had gotten the feeling the first time that the man would rather have done anything else if it meant avoiding the subject.

He waited. After a moment, Lestrade continued, "Constable Gregory used to come over for dinner every other week or so." He was staring hard at the page of his notebook. "And Collins. She worried less about me on the job after that. Says a man needs people he can trust to watch his back."

Slowly, Smith grinned. "She'd probably worry less if she knew you had some inspector friends to watch your back, I bet." He suggested brightly, looking over at Johnson, "Wouldn't you agree, Inspector?"

"I'll let Adams know." he said, shaking his head at the other man's antics. He had to admit, at least to himself, that he was impressed with Lestrade both for coming up with the idea in the first place and for being willing to face something that clearly made him uncomfortable in order to do his job. "In the meantime…"

Smith's smile was all innocence. "Stay out of trouble, I know, I know."

Kristina knew something was very, very wrong the moment her brother came through the door. She could see it in the way he moved, the blankness in his expression, and the way he could not quite meet her eyes. Something was wrong, and he was afraid to tell her exactly what.

"Out with it, Giles!" she declared, resisting the urge to reach out and shake him. It would do more harm than good at this point in their lives.

He winced, and ran a hand through his hair. "I may have invited some of the other inspectors over for dinner," he told her, and Kristina closed her eyes.

"How many?"

"Three."

"How are we going to feed them all?" Giles shrugged, miserable and at somewhat of a loss, and Kristina resisted the urge to sigh. "Does this have something to do with whatever it is that you can't talk about?" Her brother was not the sociable type. Not now, maybe not ever. Giles had known Constables Gregory and Collins for years before Kristina had met them, and that, she was fully aware, was only because she had spent those years consistently asking him if he had made any friends. She was also equally aware that neither of the two men were actually friends.

Giles nodded.

Kristina took a deep breath. "Well, it's nice to know you've got people you can trust there." She said, heading back toward the kitchen. "Go make yourself presentable." Shaking her head, she added under her breath, "It's going to be a lean week."

He heard her anyway.

At least he had someone looking out for him. She hoped.

Johnson checked the address Lestrade had written down for him yet again and wondered if the man had a death wish.

It was not, he had to admit, the worst part of town, but it was close. Johnson had kept one hand on his wallet and both eyes, as well as he could, peeled for anyone interested in getting too close. So far he had been left unmolested by potential pickpockets and thieves.

The landlady, a tired, worn-out soul, answered the door. Eyeing him suspiciously, she demanded to know what his business was.

"Here to see Lestrade." Johnson didn't waste his energy trying to be friendly.

"Second floor, door on the right," she told him wearily. "Mind yourself."

Johnson made his way up, trying to ignore the shouting and other noises behind the closed doors he passed. The inside of the building, so far, was not much better than the outside had been, but a newly promoted inspector admittedly did not make much. A constable made even less.

He found the right door and knocked. A moment later Lestrade himself answered.

"Inspector," he looked distinctly uncomfortable as he stood aside to let the other man in.

"Lestrade," Johnson stepped inside. The room was sparsely furnished, but clean. Lestrade and his sister might have been struggling, but they at least took pride in what they did have. Johnson was not surprised.

Lestrade seemed at a loss now that the man was standing inside his home instead of at the door. The older inspector took pity on him, and looked around.

"Very nice place, Lestrade, but I was under the impression there was a lady of the house, and that the entire point of this exercise was for her to meet your new friends."

Lestrade threatened to blush, then led Johnson into the kitchen.

The woman who greeted him was an uncanny imitation of her brother. Height, build, hair color – she even shared those same dark eyes that seemed to bore straight into the soul.

"Miss Lestrade," Johnson offered his hand, and the woman wiped her own hands on her apron before accepting it with an enormous smile that would have seemed improper on anyone else.

"Inspector," she greeted him cheerfully. The woman was nothing like her brother in personality. Miss Lestrade was every bit as outgoing, it seemed, as her brother was not.

"Mr. Johnson will do, Miss Lestrade," he told her, a hint of mischief in his tone. "Otherwise you might call for one inspector and end up with four."

The woman laughed and shook her head in amusement. "Well, Giles at least would know better. Still, three is a bit much when you only wanted one to begin with."

Johnson chuckled and tried to remember if he had already known Lestrade's first name, or if he had even bothered to find out. The man himself was no help; he stood useless, watching the scene play out between them as if he had no control and no desire to be involved.

A knock sounded at the door and Lestrade excused himself, leaving the two alone in the kitchen. Johnson watched him go and was certain the man looked relieved to have an escape, temporary though that reprieve might be.

He turned and realized Miss Lestrade had been watching as well, fondness and exasperation at war with each other as she stared at the now empty doorway. With a start, she seemed to come back to herself and shook her head.

Johnson remembered himself as well, and brought a parcel out from under his arm. "Mother always said it was ill manners to arrive as a guest in someone's home empty-handed."

Miss Lestrade smiled and accepted the gift, untying the paper and unwrapping the fresh loaf of bread. "Why thank you, Mr. Johnson!" she exclaimed, setting it in the center of the table. "We'll just put it here and see how long it takes my brother to notice it, shall we?" she teased, her eyes sparkling.

Her humor was infectious, and Johnson smiled back at her in spite of himself. He liked the woman, though he was still making up his mind about her brother.

Smith and Adams had predictably arrived together, Adams with a pie of some sort and Smith with a lump of butter, of all things. Johnson introduced them when it became apparent that Lestrade would not; the man seemed a bit overwhelmed with the three of them standing in his kitchen, and Johnson watched as the woman proceeded to charm both of the other inspectors as quickly as she had him.

"The table came with only the two chairs, I'm afraid, but if one of you helps Giles with the bench, and another will get the chair from his desk, I'm sure we can make do," Miss Lestrade said brightly. "Whoever's left can help me set the table."

Johnson helped Lestrade move the bench into the kitchen while Adams followed and grabbed the chair. By the time they returned, Miss Lestrade was educating a sheepish Smith on the proper way to set a table for company.

He grinned at the other inspectors as they returned. "So the knife and fork go a certain way. Who knew?"

Far from being offended, Miss Lestrade grinned and set to serving plates, briefly but firmly smacking her brother's hand out of the way when he would have gotten his own.

"You can serve yourself when we don't have company," she scolded.

Lestrade muttered something under his breath that none of his fellow inspectors caught, but made his sister nearly drop his plate. "You've been talking to Mr. Fish again, I'd wager, saying such things," she declared, then reconsidered. "Or rather, he's been talking to you. Half the building is still convinced you're a mute, Giles."

Adams snorted. Lestrade turned bright red. Unperturbed by the sight, his sister returned to her seat and served herself. "Of course, the Mullens' boy – the oldest, Giles, with all the freckles who looks like he hit a growth spurt this past month – insists he heard you not just talking, but swearing fit to shame a sailor, though no one believes him." She turned to Smith conspiratorially. "His mother told him to stop telling such tales and quit harassing poor Giles."

"And *does* he swear like a sailor, Miss Lestrade?" Smith inquired innocently while Lestrade paid careful attention to his plate.

Miss Lestrade met his gaze, her expression equally innocent except for her eyes, which glittered almost frighteningly. "I've never heard a sailor swear, Mr. Smith," she said demurely, bowing her head to study her hands as they rested briefly in her lap.

Lestrade snorted, and the other three inspectors stared. Caught, he reddened again and muttered something else under his breath that once again only his sister seemed to understand.

She laughed. "Fair enough," she agreed, as if he had spoken plainly enough for the table to hear.

Lestrade's sister was easy enough to get along with, and it was that which made dinner bearable in spite of Lestrade's utter incompetence as a host. After it was over the woman shooed them off to the other room, scolding when her brother offered to help clean up, and reminding them to take the bench and extra chair with them.

"Your sister is delightful," Adams told Lestrade as they settled down in the next room. "Are you sure you two are related?"

Lestrade forgot himself enough to glare at the man.

Johnson cleared his throat and shifted uneasily. "We need to talk, or at least make sure we're all on the same page."

"Slave traders," Adams said, turning to Smith. The other man swore.

"Are you daft, Johnson?" He demanded, and taking into account the amount of trouble Smith himself had gotten into this year alone for crossing the wrong people, Johnson had to wonder if perhaps there were some validity to the question.

"They took the Abbot boy," Lestrade spoke up. "Two more last month. Three the month before that. And those are just the ones that turned up dead."

Smith grew still. "How?" It was a question no one wanted to ask, and one Lestrade answered anyway.

"Opium. Overdose."

"Accidental, then," Adams said thoughtfully. "Someone miscalculated how much it would take to keep them docile. Either they're new to the trade, and damned incompetent, or it's a big operation, and one, two children a month means nothing to them." The man did not look happy. "You sure about this, Lestrade? Slave traders, this could mean your career. Or your life. Ours too, for that matter."

Lestrade shifted uneasily from the position he had taken by the window. His eyes were troubled, for all that his expression did not waver. Johnson wondered where he had learned to keep his feelings hidden safely behind a mask, and what exactly it had cost him.

"I don't know how to ignore it," he admitted, the words coming out slowly and cautiously. "A little boy was taken from his mother, drugged, and killed, and I don't know how to walk away from that." He leaned forward, his shoulders hunched. "How to stop seeing it."

Adams and Johnson exchanged a glance. Smith sighed. "So we take down the slave traders," he said tiredly. "Because it's what we should have been doing all along. Because we shouldn't be able to just pretend it isn't there and go about our everyday lives patting ourselves on the back for not making things worse or being as bad as the rest of them when all the time we were lying to ourselves."

Adams shifted uncomfortably in his seat. "I'm still in no hurry to get myself killed, gentlemen, so if we're going to do this, let's do it right. Clean, neat, and careful."

Seven

The question, of course, was what to do next. At Johnson's bidding, Lestrade pulled out a notebook that was starting to look ragged from the constant attention and went over everything he had collected so far, beginning with the Abbott case. His voice, as he read, remained almost too steady considering the reactions this case had provoked from him already, but perhaps by this point he had been through the dreadful words enough times that they were beginning to lose their power over him.

The gleam in his eyes as he finished and looked up disabused Johnson of any such notion. Sighing inwardly, he brought out his own notebook.

"I've been making a list of businesses that might be fronts," he explained grimly. "If anyone comes up with something I missed, they're welcome to speak up." He hesitated, then added, "And if anyone has any thoughts on how to proceed without getting killed, I'd be glad to hear them too."

The other inspectors were quiet, thinking. After a moment, Smith looked up.

"Did you ever find out about the other victims? Who they were, where they disappeared, and when?"

Adams shook his head. "That's a long shot. And a thankless job, even for us."

Smith shrugged. "We don't have much else to go on," he pointed out reasonably. "It's a lot of foot work, but maybe we can learn something in the process."

"I could go through the missing persons' files again," Lestrade offered. "And I could talk to the doctor at the morgue, see if he has any suggestions."

"Is he safe?" Adams wanted to know.

"He should be," Johnson sighed. "He's the one that brought the others to Lestrade's attention. Make sure it's a private conversation, though, and that he doesn't go around talking about it to anyone else once you're gone."

Lestrade nodded absently, writing in his notepad. Adams scowled.

"Is it a good idea to have a paper trail on this?" he asked. His scowl deepened when Johnson snorted in reply.

"Have you seen Lestrade's writing?" the inspector wanted to know. "It's all in some god-forsaken shorthand. It's unlikely anyone at the Yard could make heads or tails of it, and they'd have to get a hold of the thing first. Have you seen Lestrade's notebook sitting around without him somewhere?"

"No," Adams conceded reluctantly. "All the same, no need to get overconfident. The more precautions we take, the better." He fixed Lestrade with a glare.

The young man blinked. "Yes, sir," he responded obligingly. "It doesn't leave my person, Inspector."

"Good," Adams sniffed. Turning back to Johnson, he asked, "You trust Lestrade to do the grunt work and not run off the second he finds something?"

Johnson rolled his eyes. "More than I trust Smith, at this point." The other inspector snorted, not offended in the least.

"So let the boy do the grunt work," Smith said. "If he finds something, we can meet again after hours. In the meantime, it's probably better if Adams and I go about our business as if we knew nothing about it. You," he said to Johnson thoughtfully, "should probably make sure you have some sort of explanation ready for why Lestrade's so interested in missing persons, in case someone notices and starts asking questions.

"I'll just tell them I'm breaking the rookie in. Making sure he can follow orders, that he doesn't think he's too good for mind-numbing things like updating old files," Johnson said, far more easily than he felt.

"You could suggest it keeps him out of your way as well," Adams suggested. "Nobody likes being paired with the rookie. You may as well take advantage of that while you're at it. In the meantime, the rest of us will keep our eyes and ears open for anything that might be useful."

Lestrade made his way through the back room, maneuvering around boxes and cabinets full of old case notes and files and wondered why missing persons' cases were stored in the back of the room. He also wondered when the last time the room itself had been organized; it was plain enough that the room was used mostly as a dumping ground for old paperwork.

He tucked himself into a corner and considered the drawer that was the Yard's missing persons' file. The reports were lazily written, haphazardly stored. There were also shockingly few considering the number of years spanned in that drawer.

By now he could have rattled off the names and ages, when they had actually been taken down, of most of the people on that list. The realization was not encouraging.

Frowning to himself, Lestrade set aside any reports made in the last five years that matched the description of the six children who had been killed. After a moment's consideration, he started another set, this of any other children who had gone missing during that time. Frowning, he then sorted out any older reports of children matching those who had been killed.

He spent the morning carefully copying the information from each stack into his notebook, making note of how they were organized for later use. It was nearly noon when he finally finished, tucking his notebook into his jacket pocket, and returned the files to their drawer. Standing and brushing off any dust that had managed to accumulate on his trousers while he worked, he allowed himself to hope he would not have to come back here again anytime soon.

Stopping to check in with Inspector Johnson on his way out, Lestrade left Scotland Yard and headed back to the morgue.

Dr. Holdsworth looked up from his desk in surprise. Rising quickly, he crossed the room. "Inspector, Lestrade, was it?" He asked, shaking the man's hand. He received a nod in confirmation from the inspector. "What can I do for you? I'll admit I wasn't expecting to see you again."

Lestrade stepped into the doctor's office and tried to sort out what to say next. "I came to ask if you remembered anything else about the..." he hesitated, looking for the right words. "If there were anything about the bodies that didn't make it into the files. Or anything that stood out to you." He shifted uneasily. "If you have the time, that is."

Holdsworth took a moment to study the other man. "It wasn't just a coincidence, then," he said, seeing confirmation in the inspector's dark eyes. Sighing, he returned to his seat, waving Lestrade to a chair across the desk from his own. Rubbing his temple absently, he closed his eyes and tried to bring the files and the children involved to mind.

"I'm not sure what I can tell you that wasn't already in their files." He admitted, feeling weary. "You do think they're connected then, I take it?"

Lestrade did not answer. Instead he flipped to a page in his notebook and considered the writing on it. "The first was a young girl?" he asked instead.

Holdsworth shuddered slightly. "Couldn't have been more than ten years of age." He said. "No sign of violence. She was fed, cared for, up until she died." He leaned back in his chair, his eyes distant. "The second was a boy. Younger, maybe a year younger. Same as the girl. No sign of violence. Clean, fed, cared for, except for being dead. The others were the same."

Lestrade frowned at his notebook. "They were all well-fed?" he asked at last. "All healthy?"

"Except for being dead," the doctor agreed, then caught himself. "The second girl looked as if she had recently been unwell, but was recovering. Either she had been sick and was getting better, or had been underfed but was gaining weight."

Lestrade considered this. "How long would something like that take?" he asked.

Holdsworth shrugged. "It depends on how unwell she was before. Children generally bounce back faster than adults, but now that I think about it, I would say it's likely that she had been like that for a while, and that she had only recently begun to put on weight." He pursed his lips, thinking. "Either she had been sick for some time and was recovering, or she had grown up in a home with very little food on the table, and was recently beginning to make up for it."

Lestrade turned to a fresh page in his notebook and began writing. "And the others?" He asked.

Holdsworth shook his head. "I can't say for certain," he admitted.

"Anything else you can think of?" Lestrade asked, looking up. "Anything at all?"

Holdsworth shook his head once more. "Nothing else comes to mind," he said. "I am sorry, Inspector."

Lestrade stood. "It's more than I had before I came here," he pointed out, though both men knew it was little enough. "Thank you."

The doctor stood as well. "I'll let you know if I think of anything else," he offered.

Lestrade nodded absently and excused himself, leaving Dr. Holdsworth to frown thoughtfully at the inspector's retreating back as he made his way down the hall.

He wondered idly how long the man would last as a policeman; it was a job every bit as brutal as his own, if not more so.

Lestrade realized with a jolt that he had been walking as he thought, and that he had not been paying much attention to where he was going as he did so. Fully aware that such a lapse could easily get him killed, he looked around to get his bearings.

The market where the Abbott boy had been taken. Lestrade let out a breath he hadn't realized he was holding and stood still for a moment, watching as people came and went.

The hair on the back of his neck prickled; Lestrade turned and realized he was being watched. Meeting his eyes, the vendor waved. Lestrade made his way over to the stall.

"Mr. Richards," he greeted the man. He received a smile in return.

"Inspector Lestrade," he replied. The smile faded. "Shame, what happened with the Abbott boy," he offered. "Poor Harold deserved better."

"I'm sure he did." Lestrade replied absently, then asked. "Do children go missing often around here, Mr. Richards?"

The vendor thought for a moment, then shook his head. "It's pretty safe for families, women, the little ones. That's why she brought him here, you know. It was supposed to be safe."

"So you don't know of any other children going missing while here with their families?" Lestrade's voice lowered so the other man had to strain to hear him.

"You want somewhere children go missing all the time, Mr. Lestrade, you want to try some of the poorer parts of the city. Folks go missing there every day."

Lestrade sighed. "Thank you anyway, Mr. Richards. I appreciate your time."

Richards smiled again. "Take care, Inspector. And your sister."

Eight

Lestrade returned home that evening to find Kristina sitting on the couch, holding one of the neighbors as the woman cried into her shoulder. He paused uncertainly by the door, and both women looked up at him, the neighbor with red-rimmed eyes. Kristina herself looked nearly ready to cry.

Lestrade knew well enough when his presence was not wanted; years of experience told him that the best thing he could do at the current moment was get out of the way. He hung up his coat and excused himself, making his way to the kitchen.

It looked as if the woman had been here for some time. Kristina had not even started dinner. Shrugging, Lestrade rolled up his sleeves. Setting the tea kettle to boil, he looked around for some clue of what his sister had planned to make. It was not as if the man were completely incompetent in the kitchen himself.

He had finished chopping up vegetables by the time the kettle started singing. Setting aside the blade carefully – Kristina kept all her knives dangerously sharp – he fixed a cup for both Kristina and the neighbor and returned to the living room only long enough to disperse them.

He resumed cooking, not quite willing to admit to himself that perhaps the distraction was a good thing – it was the first real break his mind had gotten from the case since they had found the boy in the morgue. It was hardly safe to let his mind wander while chopping vegetables, and Kristina would never let him hear the end of it if he burnt dinner. As far as she was concerned, thinking about a case would never be an acceptable excuse.

Carrots, potatoes, and onions would roast nicely alongside the chicken, and while dinner would be late, it would also be much appreciated. Lestrade had been hungry before – they both had – and waiting a few hours longer than had become usual was hardly a trial.

He fixed his own cup of tea and looked around. Dishes needed, done; the floor, swept. The day's mending still sat on the table. Kristina had spent most of the day with the woman, Lestrade realized.

He finished his tea and set about tidying up the kitchen while keeping an eye on dinner. The mending could wait until they had eaten, he supposed. There was not much of it there. He supposed it could reasonably wait until tomorrow, but Kristina would likely not sleep tonight, knowing it was unfinished. The woman hated to leave things undone.

Lestrade supposed it was a trait the two shared.

Kristina came in with the two cups. Setting them in the sink, she looked around. "I'm sorry about dinner, Giles," she said. "Sarah's been here for most of the day. The little one ran out in front of a cab..." The woman trailed off, staring blankly at nothing. "I can't imagine."

Lestrade checked the chicken simply for something to do. "I can cook, Kristina," he reminded her, his voice soft. It was not what he meant to say, but the woman would understand anyway.

She smiled. "I'm going to take her home and try to get her settled. See if there's anything I can do to help. You may have to fend for yourself for the night, at least." Her eye fell on the basket of mending. "Leave that. I'll take care of it before bed."

Lestrade shrugged instead of arguing. He could do as he pleased once she was gone. "Take all the time you need," he said instead.

She pulled him into a hug without warning, holding him tight and resting her forehead briefly on his shoulder. When she let him go it was with a sigh and a rueful smile.

Lestrade ate dinner alone. Cleaning up took very little time, so he sat back down at the table with the basket of clothes and got to work. There were a few of his shirts, one with a button that had come off, and several of her dresses. None of the tears were particularly difficult to stitch, and were mercifully not located anywhere obvious. Lestrade set to work with needle and thread, making sure to keep the stitches neat, tiny, and even.

The chore finished, Lestrade wondered if he were supposed to wait up for his sister. He was pretty sure that she was not supposed to be out unchaperoned, but less certain how that rule applied when it came to comforting neighboring women in one's own building. He was also fully aware that his sister could take care of herself and was quite likely to laugh off such concerns, if he brought them up.

He settled on the couch, content to doze until she came in.

Lestrade started awake several hours later. Kristina stood frozen in front of him, eyes wide, looking for all the world like a child caught in mischief. The room was dark and far too quiet.

"Sorry." Her voice came out hushed. Seeing Lestrade move, she added, "Don't get up. I'm perfectly capable of fending for myself, Giles."

He leaned back, and she disappeared into the other room. He could hear her footsteps, and the clinking of glass and of utensils, as she got herself some dinner.

Instead of eating at the table she returned to the living room and sat next to him, balancing a plate in her lap. For a while she ate in silence, too weary to offer much in the way of conversation after such a day.

"Took longer than I thought for her to cry herself to sleep," she admitted. She offered no resistance when her brother went to take her empty plate. Amused, she leaned back and rolled her shoulders back to take the stiffness out of them. "I would have been home sooner, but none of the other children had been looked after, and getting them taken care of took some time."

Lestrade took the dishes to the kitchen and returned to sit beside her once more. For a long time they sat like that, in the near-dark and not-quite stillness of the room.

"Let's go, Lestrade." Adams popped his head into the office only for it to disappear from view immediately after delivering the summons. Lestrade hesitated only long enough for the other man to call back, "We don't have time to wait for Johnson."

The younger inspector followed the older one down the hall, through Scotland Yard, and out into the street. Once there, Adams flung out an arm to wave down a cab. Only once they had climbed inside and were on their way did he explain.

"Constables found a doctor murdered in the back alley behind the morgue," Adams said, and Lestrade felt his blood run cold. "Holdsworth. That was yours, wasn't he?"

Lestrade did not answer.

"Lestrade?"

The man blinked as if pulling himself back to the present.

"Holdsworth, yes," he agreed. "I spoke to him yesterday. He was the one who mentioned the other children to me in the first place." Lestrade looked a little lost. Adams almost felt sorry for him.

"Think he started digging, looking for more information?" Adams asked. "Maybe asked the wrong question? Or talked to the wrong person?" He frowned. "Or maybe someone noticed a policeman coming around one too many times for comfort and got nervous."

Adams looked thoughtful. "Maybe he found something else and got killed for it. Tell you what, Lestrade. Why don't you go have a look around his office before you join me in looking over the body? See if anything looks out of place."

"Yes, sir," Lestrade nodded briskly. He seemed to have recovered himself, though there was something in the set of his jaw that Adams did not care for at all.

When they reached the morgue Adams got out first and made his way back to the alley. Lestrade turned and went inside the building as directed. By now he knew the way to the dead man's office well enough to find it without help.

The room had been ransacked. Where the doctor's office had been a contradiction with piles and piles of paper and files stacked almost neatly on every surface, now it looked as if someone had opened a window and let a strong wind have its way. Everything had been scattered. Drawers hung half opened. Very little of the floor could be seen peeking through a carpet of paper.

Lestrade stared at the mess and debated whether to leave the mess or start going through it. Holdsworth had obviously died outside. Someone had been through the office, likely looking for something. Going through the room might offer some idea of what the killer – or accomplice – had been searching for.

Maybe the doctor had found something.

Or, more likely, someone thought he was spending too much time talking to the police and wanted to make sure he had not.

Lestrade let out a deep breath and knelt in the doorway to examine those papers lying closest to him. As far as he could tell, none of them contained information important to his case; just day-to-day paperwork completed, half-completed, or waiting to be filed away.

He stood and looked around the office once more, this time for something that was not so much out of place as for something that did not belong in the room at all.

He found nothing. Backing out into the hall, he pulled the door closed and went to join Adams.

On his way he stopped and reassigned a constable to guard the murdered man's office. "No one goes in unless it's me or Inspector Adams," he said.

The constable saluted. "Yes, Inspector."

Adams waved Lestrade over as he reached the back alley. "Let's see what you make of the body," he said.

The two inspectors knelt beside the murdered man.

Holdsworth lay face down, his head bare, a bloody gash opened in the back of his head. Lestrade stared at the wound unseeingly for a moment, then found his focus.

"Hit from behind," he murmured. "Either someone sneaked up behind him, or he knew the murderer and turned his back on him." Lestrade looked around for some suggestion as to which it had been. Seeing nothing of use, he turned his attention back to the wound. "That looks like whatever hit him had a sharp edge to it," he said, his eyes narrowing. "Turn him over?"

Adams helped him, and together the two inspectors looked the dead man over.

"No other injuries," Lestrade offered after a moment. "Nothing to suggest he tried to protect himself."

Adams scowled. "Probably didn't know he was being attacked until he was already dead."

Lestrade looked around the back alley. "Somebody searched his office. Papers everywhere. I set a constable to make sure no one else went in."

Adams sighed. "We'll search his office next, then," he said. "Maybe we'll get lucky."

After they finished examining the body, Lestrade led Adams back inside the building and to Holdsworth's office. Adams dismissed the constable and opened the door. Taking one brief look around the room, he turned to Lestrade.

"Go through *everything*. Straighten up when you're done. I'm going to go convince whoever's in charge that not only will he be doing me a favor by keeping you out of my hair for a couple hours, but that he'll also benefit: He won't have to find someone on staff to do the clean-up." Adams grinned. "We'll have a nice laugh about you looking for clues," he said.

Lestrade set to work without arguing. Adams left him to it.

Nine

It took Lestrade the remainder of the morning and part of the afternoon to restore some semblance of order to the deceased doctor's office. Part of it was due to the sheer number of papers strewn about. Most of it was the fact that Lestrade stopped to at least skim through each and every file he came across.

Anything that looked remotely interesting went into its own rapidly growing stack in the corner. Everything else went neatly stacked on the desk, then on the doctor's chair, then on the guest chair. When he ran out of flat surfaces he started using the corner behind the desk.

Any drawers that had been pulled out, whether from the desk or the filing cabinet, came under examination as well. It was slow, dull work.

His head throbbed by the time he finished. His eyes felt dry and a rather like a bit of dirt had gotten in them. With a barely audible sigh he turned his attention to the first stack and picked up the top file. Opening it, he began to skim through its contents.

Two hours later Lestrade was forced to come to the conclusion that there was absolutely nothing useful in Holdsworth's office. The man had not been killed after learning some terrible secret.

He had simply been seen talking to the wrong person. Namely, Lestrade.

Lestrade ignored the sympathy in Johnson's eyes as he reported back to the inspector and shared with him the events of the day. Or tried to. The other man made it difficult.

"You can't blame yourself," Johnson told him, resisting the urge to lay a reassuring hand on the man's shoulder. "He chose to get involved when he decided to bring the children to your attention in the first place. He had to have realized he was putting himself in danger. What happened is not your fault."

Lestrade thought that, at least, debatable, but knew better than to argue.

"What now?" he asked. The alternative was to wallow in pity, and he had little interest in that.

Johnson rubbed his face with his hands. "Do we have an autopsy on Holdsworth yet?"

"He was hit in the back of the head with a heavy object that had at least one sharp edge. Crushed the back of the skull, caused a lot of bleeding in the process," Lestrade replied. "No other injuries. Happened sometime late last night, most likely after midnight."

Johnson let out a long sigh. "Damn."

He looked up. Lestrade was going through his notebook again, as if the answer were already written down somewhere and he just needed to keep looking until he found it.

The older inspector wished it were that easy.

"I suppose it's too much to hope for that someone saw Holdsworth that night? Or whoever he met with? Or thought something seemed off about him that day?"

Lestrade snapped his notebook closed. "Adams did the questioning. He said nobody admitted to seeing anything. Nobody noticed anything out of the ordinary."

Johnson ran a hand through his hair. "Well, for now, it's his case. We're treating it as unrelated, which is better for us if someone's getting nervous enough to kill him for talking to us."

Lestrade looked away.

"It had to be someone that saw us together," he said.

"Unless he was asking questions and someone caught wind," Johnson pointed out. "Adams probably already checked, but I'll mention it to him when I get a chance." The man was quiet for a moment, thinking.

"We need to be very careful from here on out. This does not get discussed outside of this office. Don't talk to the others any more than you have to – it's suspicious for them to pay so much attention to such new blood. I'll update them as necessary." He looked Lestrade over critically.

"We'll keep our heads down for a day or two anyway, just to be on the safe side. And you do nothing without me." He held out a hand before the other man could protest. "We don't need you going off and getting yourself killed, Lestrade. You've got too much potential, and I've put too much work into you already. We take it slow, take it safe, at least for as long as possible, and maybe, just maybe, we might make it through this alive and with our careers intact."

Lestrade turned to stare out the window, but did not argue.

Johnson stifled a sigh. The man standing before him was one of the most infuriating people he had ever had to work with in his entire career, and one of the most difficult. At the same time, there was something about the way Lestrade operated that demanded respect, however grudgingly given. It was clear that the man took his job seriously, and was not afraid of either hard work or of putting himself in difficult and dangerous situations in order to do what he believed was right.

With time, experience, and a little seasoning, he would make an excellent inspector. With luck, he might go far in his chosen profession. If he lived.

Johnson silently promised himself that he would do everything within his power to make sure Lestrade lived long enough to prove himself.

They spent the rest of the afternoon catching up on the paperwork that, no matter how much time they spent on it, always seemed to creep up and threaten to completely overwhelm them. It helped Johnson get his mind off their current obsession, but it was painfully obvious at only a glance that it did not have the same effect on Lestrade. If anything, the younger man seemed to grow more restless with every passing report.

Not that he said anything. Or that he allowed it to affect the quality of his work. Each form was filled out slowly, carefully, and meticulously in neat and tiny handwriting that seemed completely at odds with his usual shorthand.

Neither inspector was very happy at the end of the day. Johnson sent Lestrade home with a wave of his hand and a reminder, one he was almost certain the man did not need, to be careful. Better to give an unnecessary warning than to assume and have Lestrade turn up dead the following morning.

Johnson watched the younger man leave the office, shoulders stiff, body tense with a nervous energy, and admitted to himself that he had, somehow, started to like Lestrade, even if it was just a little bit. How that had happened, he had absolutely no idea.

Kristina recognized her brother's mood the second he came through the door. Nonetheless, she offered him a cheerful (enough) greeting that he did not reciprocate and likely would not remember later. Shoving away a burst of exasperation, she caught him by the elbow and all but corralled him into the kitchen before he could get distracted and forget to eat.

Dinner was a grim, silent affair. For once, Kristina did not bother trying to hold a conversation – Giles would neither appreciate nor notice her efforts. Instead she resigned herself to making sure he ate. When she rose to clear the table, he came to himself enough to help, but remained silent – almost surly, really over the sink full of dishes.

Kristina set the kettle to boiling as he settled distractedly at the table and pulled out his notebook yet again. A stray glance revealed nearly illegible writing, and the woman shook her head and busied herself making tea for them both.

He noticed enough to thank her when she brought him a cup, and Kristina decided to take what she could get.

She loved her brother dearly, but he was not an easy man to live with. Not because he was careless, or ill-tempered, or anything of that sort.

No, Giles was difficult because if anything he was too cautious. Too reserved. If he were angry or otherwise upset, he tended to lock the emotion down tight rather than risk letting it show. And anything that made him feel vulnerable – well, it only made him withdraw even farther. Even around Kristina he rarely allowed himself to relax.

It was a product of his upbringing, the woman well knew. Life before London, especially childhood, had been a special kind of hell for Giles, and there had been little enough Kristina had been able to do about it. She understood why her brother was the way he was and could hardly blame him for it.

He had survived their upbringing, but that did not mean he had escaped it unscathed. If anything she was surprised, sometimes, at how well he held himself together.

It did not make it any easier to watch him now.

She wondered, sometimes, if time and a sense of self, separate from all that had been practically forced on him in his youth, would eventually allow him to relax, just a little. Find people who would accept him for who he was. She also wondered if maybe, just maybe, one day he might be able to do the same himself.

Kristina shook her head and rose from the table. She bid her brother a good night he likely also did not hear and went to bed. There was nothing else she could do for him at the moment.

He did not answer. She did not expect a reply, not least because he rarely trusted himself to speak when in such a mood, even if he had not been so wrapped up in whatever it was at work that had him so upset. He would not risk saying something to her that he would regret later.

Lestrade sat at the table long into the night, trying to find something – anything – that might help him figure out what to do next.

"I want to look into the rest of our missing persons cases," Lestrade told Johnson the next morning. "Talk to the people who made the reports: parents, siblings, other family members. Starting with the most recent, and especially any that match the description of the Abbot boy and the other children."

Johnson looked up at him from his desk. "You realize no one is going to want to talk to you."

"I know."

"You may not even find anyone to talk to. People move. People disappear."

"I know."

"And even if you do find someone and they do agree to talk to you, there's no particular reason what they say has to be the truth."

"I know." Lestrade looked almost rumpled – for him. The other inspector wondered if he had gotten any sleep the night before.

Johnson debated the request, trying to gauge how much trouble the younger man could get into on his own against the knowledge that he was slightly more likely to get a response if he went alone. One policeman was bad enough. If they both went, they wouldn't get so much as a word out of anyone.

Lestrade could hold his own in a fight, the older Inspector had seen that much. But how much help that would be if someone caught on to what he was doing was another thing entirely. If they attracted the wrong attention on this, Lestrade would be dead before he even knew it.

Still, it was something the other man could do.

"Go ahead," Johnson gave permission. "But be careful. London is hostile enough without trying to find slave traders. Tread softly. And if, by some miracle, you do find something out, you come straight back to me to report. No wandering off on your own on a hunch, no checking up on something someone told you. You come to me with anything you learn. Understood?"

Lestrade nodded and excused himself. Johnson watched him go, his heart beating rapidly in his chest and an odd sense of foreboding sending a shiver down his spine.

In the poorer part of the city, at least, it was incredibly difficult to find those who had once taken the time to go to the police about missing people. As Johnson had suggested, some had moved, and some had simply disappeared.

Very few of their neighbors were interested in explaining what had occurred, or in talking to Lestrade at all. Door after door after door closed in his face. And when he did find one of the names mentioned in the old reports, the results were the same.

Lestrade pressed on, refusing to give up before he had at least attempted to contact everyone involved in filling out the missing persons' reports. In some way it was better than simply doing nothing, even if his chances of learning anything useful were incredibly slim.

He turned and caught a small hand as it reached for his pocket, the hand's owner supposing that Lestrade had been too preoccupied with his thoughts to notice he was being shadowed. Their eyes met. The boy started to struggle.

Lestrade took in the far too thin child in ragged clothing before him and let go. "Off with you, then," he murmured, and the boy, not needing to be told twice, took off.

Lestrade watched him disappear around the corner. Sighing, he turned and made his way back down the street.

It took several fruitless days to work his way through his list. At the end of it, aside from perhaps a more intimate knowledge of the poorer sections of London (and certainly a better eye for trouble from would-be pickpockets), Lestrade had gained little for his trouble other than tired, aching feet and a deeper frustration at the distrust for London's policeman held by its people. He was no closer to finding any answers. No closer to figuring out who had kidnapped and murdered those children, and no closer to putting a stop to it.

Johnson would have offered encouragement, had there been any to offer. He had known from the start that it would be an all-but-useless endeavor, but lacking any better alternatives, had thought it best to go ahead and let the younger man go. Now he wondered if he had made the right choice.

He did not know how much more the man currently standing before him could take.

Ten

Kristina met her brother at the door that evening. "We have guests," she said in an undertone. "I hope I haven't made a mistake letting them in, when I asked what they wanted, they looked almost as cagey as you do when I ask about work."

In a louder voice, she continued, "You remember Mr. Richards, from the marketplace, Giles? He brought a friend, a young lady. Miss...?" Kristina trailed off in a way that told Lestrade it was not the first attempt she had made at learning the woman's name.

Looking from one man to the other, Kristina reconsidered. "I'll put some tea on, leave you three to talk. Will you be staying for dinner, Mr. Richards?"

The market vendor shook his head. "No, thank you, Miss Lestrade. My Millie would never let me hear the end of it, helping myself to someone else's cooking."

They shared a laugh, and Kristina excused herself. Lestrade, not entirely certain what had brought the other man to his home (never mind how the man knew where he lived), made his way carefully into the room.

The amusement was gone from Richards' face. "Forgive me for taking the liberty, Inspector," he apologized, "but our meeting the other day got me to thinking some, after you'd left."

Lestrade grimaced, but the other man went on. "You asked about other children going missing, and I thought at first you were just new to the position and trying to be sure you'd done everything you were supposed to with little

Harold." He licked his lips nervously. "But I got to talking it over with Millie later, and she asked some questions, and well, maybe I reconsidered that opinion some."

Richards looked far more serious than Lestrade had ever seen him.

"And then I thought, begging your pardon, Inspector, but I thought, I've known you and your sister since you first showed up in London, you looking like some sort of devil was after you, and you've always struck me as a decent sort. A good man." Lestrade shifted uncomfortably but did not interrupt.

"And I thought, you didn't seem the kind to change that, just because you became an inspector. So maybe you're a bit different from some of the others, and maybe you're asking about others disappearing because you actually care about what happens to the youngsters. And the more I thought it, the more I was sure I had the right of it." Here he turned and looked at his companion.

"I also got to thinking that Harold was a beautiful little boy, Inspector. The kind that everyone loves. The kind that if he'd been born to more fortunate parents would probably never been let out of their sight, even for a second."

Lestrade did not react, but Richards had known the man long enough to know he knew when to cut an already too long speech short.

"I thought I'd take a risk, Inspector. This lady, I don't want to put her in danger if I'm wrong by giving her name, but this lady has a beautiful little girl, about nine years old, Inspector. Blonde hair, blue eyes, prettiest smile you ever did see."

Something clicked in the inspector's eyes. Richards nodded. "Someone tried to grab her, about four months ago. Tried to snatch her right out of her mother's grip."

Lestrade looked over at the woman. "Tried?" He repeated. The woman nodded. Not meeting his eyes, she fidgeted with her skirt.

"I know she's that pretty, Inspector. I keep a bit of ribbon tied to her wrist, and mine, so she can't wander off." Looking to Richards for encouragement, she continued. "I felt a tug, and heard her scream, but he didn't get her. Nearly pulled my arm off, it felt like, but he didn't get her. The knot held."

Lestrade reached for his notebook. "Did you see the man who tried to take her?" he asked.

The woman struggled for a moment, making up her mind, then nodded. "I did. I can tell you what he looked like, what he was wearing, everything. It's not something I'll ever forget, or my daughter either. She won't even go outside anymore."

Lestrade opened his notebook. "Whenever you're ready, ma'am."

Lestrade was silent as he worked through his dinner, but this was a different sort of silence than Kristina had become accustomed to over the past few days. Her brother was not lost, or frustrated, or trying, albeit somewhat unsuccessfully, to bide his time until he had pieced together enough of the puzzle before him to take action.

No, Giles had enough to act on – whatever it was he was working on. Enough knowledge to make a choice. Now he was struggling with the decision itself, weighing each individual issue before he acted.

He snapped back to the present abruptly, and finished his dinner. Whatever it was, the decision had been made. For better or worse, all that was left now was for Giles to act.

He rose from the table. "I'm going out," he said. "Don't wait up for me."

He kissed her on the cheek before leaving, and Kristina allowed herself to relax. Whatever happened next, it would happen quickly, and on the streets, at least, she knew her brother was more than capable of taking care of himself.

Lestrade settled into a seat at the bar as if he did so every night of the week, and without seeming to pay any mind to the room full of people behind him. Any visible discomfort at having his back exposed was currently limited to a tightness around his eyes. Willie saw him enter and did not miss the way his gaze regularly drifted up to the mirrored strip on the wall above the liquor shelves-the same mirrored strip he himself used to keep an eye on the room when his own back was turned. The bar's owner chuckled to himself and wondered when he had started to take an interest in the young man.

Willie took his time making his way over; Lestrade certainly did not seem to be in any hurry. When he did stop in front of the newly promoted inspector, he offered the man a smile.

"Good evening, Mr. Lestrade. I take it nobody else has managed to do ya in since I saw you last?" He asked, reaching for a glass.

Lestrade shook his head, "Not yet, I'm afraid, Mr. Williams." The lad could be polite to a fault, Willie had noticed, but he had never gotten the impression that it was out of weakness.

"What can I do for ya, laddie?" The older man asked, keeping his tone friendly. Something in the younger man's eyes told him Lestrade had not come simply for a drink. He wondered if he were about to change his long-standing philosophy on keeping out of the affairs of his customers.

Lestrade looked distinctly uncomfortable. "The usual, please, and I wondered," here he faltered. "I wondered if we might *talk*, when you have a moment."

Willie grinned openly at the man. "Tired of trailing along after the other inspectors and being talked at like ya know nothing of the business, I'd wager." He doubted the inspector had come simply for gossip, but no one else needed to know that. "Stick around, I'll be back when I can."

Lestrade was content to wait until the night had dwindled and all that remained were those who needed rousting from their spots and sent on home. The young man sat seemingly lost in his thoughts as Willie cleared the last of the room and said goodnight to the serving girls.

Lights dimmed, doors locked, Willie poured two drinks and went to sit down across from the new inspector.

"Now what's on your mind, Mr. Lestrade?" he asked, his tone friendly enough. "Not that I can promise anything more than a friendly ear."

"I know you make it a habit not to get involved in other people's business." Lestrade studied his drink. With his eyes downcast, it was that much more difficult to tell what he was thinking.

Willie leaned back in his chair. "Or to get attached, but here we are." He shrugged. "I *like* you, Mr. Lestrade. Lord only knows why."

As Willie expected, the other man did not take offense. For a while both men were silent, one waiting, the other in thought.

"I ask only that you hear me out," Lestrade said at last, "and, should you decide you want nothing to do with it, your silence. But I came here looking for a name, with only a description that may or may not be accurate. I thought if anyone might recognize him, it would be you."

"Quite a speech," Willie grunted. Polite or no, the lad had never been much of a talker. Apparently that was by preference rather than necessity. "Perhaps you'd better give me some idea of what you want this man for, since you're asking me to give his name up to a policeman, and as far as I know, all he's done is possibly come into my bar."

This time Lestrade smiled, though it was entirely without humor. "The last man I asked for help was murdered."

Willie shrugged that off. "I'm more than capable of handling myself, Mr. Lestrade, though maybe I should ask before this goes any further how you know *you* can trust me, all things considered."

Lestrade shrugged. "I don't *know*," he admitted.

"*He doesn't like not knowing,*" Willie thought to himself. Taking a generous sip of his drink, he beckoned for the man to continue.

"If I'm wrong, I very likely won't survive the night."

Lestrade did not look worried by the admission.

"*Not afraid of death, that one,*" the older man thought.

"So what tales of danger and death bring you to me of all people for help?" Willie asked, sobering.

By the time Lestrade had given him a rough outline of the situation, leaving out the involvement of the other inspectors as well as the names of anyone else he had spoken to (it was one thing to risk his own life; putting others in danger over nothing more than a *feeling* was unthinkable), the other man was positively grim.

"Slave traders," Willie breathed. "You *have* put your foot in it." He was silent a moment, thinking. "If it were anything else, Inspector, I'd refuse," he told Lestrade. The other man nodded as if he had expected exactly that response.

Willie finished the rest of his drink in one go, wondering what he was getting himself into. Setting the empty glass on the bar and wiping his mouth with the back of his hand, he met Lestrade's dark eyes.

"Give me the description."

Johnson wished he could revel in having made it to his own office before Lestrade, but the infrequency with which such an occurrence had happened in the past combined with the case they were currently (secretly) working only served to make him nervous instead. It did not help that Smith and Adams were both accounted for, and that neither had seen the rookie inspector that morning.

There was nothing he could do but wait, however, but

keep reminding himself that the man was not even late. If it had been any other person under any other circumstances, he would likely not even have noticed.

As it was, he had almost convinced himself that Lestrade was dead in a gutter somewhere when the younger inspector arrived, alive and unharmed and just two minutes before he was officially due.

"Sorry I'm late, sir," Lestrade murmured distractedly. Johnson waited, but received no explanation, and aside from the fact that Lestrade was refusing to meet his eyes, there was a stiffness in his back and shoulders that said the other man was under no inclination to give one.

Annoyed, Johnson put him to work in the back room, cleaning and organizing papers that had likely not been touched since they had first been filed. The room itself had never been cleaned, as far as he knew.

It was busywork, but Lestrade needed to be kept busy. He also, it seemed, needed a reminder that he was still the rookie inspector and Johnson was the one with experience.

If it kept him out of harm's way and from asking questions about slave traders for a day or two while he and Adams tried to figure out *what,* exactly had gotten Dr. Holdsworth killed and who, if anybody, knew what they were investigating, all the better.

Lestrade was not going to die today. Not on Johnson's watch.

Lestrade did not argue, but set to work almost meekly. This reaction worried Johnson even more, and he went to go make himself a cup of tea before he lost his temper with the younger man.

He relented and brought one back for Lestrade as well, setting it on one of the few clear surfaces in the room. "It doesn't have to all be done today," he told the other inspector. "There's plenty of time." When Lestrade paused and looked at him uncertainly, he gestured toward the mug.

"Are you always this socially inept, or just when it suits your purpose?" he asked conversationally as Lestrade stopped working and considered his tea.

"Sir?"

Johnson sighed. "Your instincts are good," he explained. "When it comes to asking questions, looking for information. That takes some understanding of people. And I've seen you have conversations. You seemed to get along with Willie well enough."

Lestrade was carefully staring into his cup as if it were the only thing of interest in the world.

Johnson shook his head. "And when you're wrapped up in your work, you seem confident, like you know what you're doing. But now, for instance. You act like you've never so much as talked to another human before. Like you don't know what to expect."

He stopped short of asking any of the actual questions floating around in his mind and waited, watching the other man.

Lestrade looked up, his eyes guarded.

"What people say and what people mean are not always the same thing," he said at last, slowly, as if trying to put a complicated idea into words. "And their thoughts are not always clear in their actions. Sometimes it's easy enough to see, other times not." He set his cup down.

"And sometimes even if I understand what someone *means,* I don't always know how to answer." Lestrade hesitated. "When I was younger it was safer – easier not to say anything.

"But here there are rules. Procedures. If I learn them, I know what do. How to react. I know what is the law, and what's against it. It's clear. Easy."

Johnson laughed. "Only you would suggest that our job is *easy* just because you know what the law says we should be doing. "

Lestrade frowned. "Easy isn't the right word," he admitted. "I'm not sure what the right one is, if it exists. But I know where I stand, here. I don't always know that anywhere else."

He looked away, uncomfortable, and Johnson wondered how much it had cost him, to admit so much.

"Not used to being vulnerable around people either, are you?" he asked. "Safer to keep to yourself?"

Lestrade did not deny it.

Johnson kept Lestrade working in the back room for the rest of the day. When he finally waved for the man to set aside what he was doing and go home, they were both well tired of the affair, though Lestrade had predictably not so much as uttered a word in complaint.

Lestrade stood up and turned as if to go. Stopping in the doorway, he looked back at the older inspector. Johnson resisted the urge to swear as he got a good look at the other man's expression.

"I was wondering, Inspector, whether you were doing anything this evening?" Lestrade's tone was almost light, almost casual, and somehow completely missing the mark.

Johnson scowled and nodded in response – not to the question Lestrade had actually asked, but the one he had meant. It took all his willpower not to demand immediately to know what the hell the other man had been up to – and when.

He dragged Lestrade home with *him* this time – his wife was visiting with her mother, as she often did when he was in what she called one of his "moods." There would be plenty of privacy there, and he would not have to deal with the painful spectacle of Lestrade trying to figure out what to do with a co-worker in his house.

The house was quiet when they arrived.

"Make yourself at home," Johnson grunted, busying himself with making the living room presentable. Sarah had been gone almost as long as one rookie inspector had been making his life miserable. "Tea?"

Lestrade startled at the offer, and it occurred to Johnson to wonder why his sister had not taken him in hand when she certainly seemed sociable enough. He shrugged the thought away quickly; surely the woman had her reasons.

Eleven

"Since you're obviously still alive and unhurt, let's skip the lecture. This time." Johnson stretched out in his chair in front of the fire.

Lestrade sat primly at the edge of a matching chair and met the other man's eyes without so much as a hint of either guilt or shame. "Mr. Richards was waiting for me when I got home from work yesterday," he said without preamble. "He had a friend with him. A woman. Someone tried to take her daughter about four months ago and failed."

Johnson took a sip of his tea. "The daughter was pretty?" he asked.

"Blonde hair. Blue eyes. Nine years old," Lestrade confirmed.

"Go on,"

"She gave me a description of the man."

"Accurate?"

"As far as I could tell." Here Lestrade paused, almost looking away. He knew Johnson would not like what he had to say next.

"Spit it out, Lestrade."

"I went to Willie's after dinner," Lestrade said. Johnson had a feeling he had gone for more than just a drink. "I spoke to him, after the bar closed."

"You asked him for help?" Johnson couldn't decide whether to be angry or impressed.

Lestrade shrugged. "I didn't mention any other names. If I were wrong, I would be the only one to suffer for it."

"Well, you're not dead, yet. At any rate, did he actually agree to help? Willie never gets involved with anything, and especially not police business. He doesn't even like us!"

"He doesn't like slave traders," Lestrade offered. "He agreed to listen to the description the mother gave me."

"And?" Johnson pressed, when Lestrade did not immediately continue.

"And he gave me a name." Lestrade suddenly looked miserable. "Said that the clothes the woman described weren't how he usually dressed, but that he had seen the man dressed that way himself a time or two, thinking no one would recognize him. Said it always struck him as odd."

"Stop dithering, Lestrade, it's not like you," Johnson said, when the other man fell silent again. "If we've got a name, that's farther than I ever expected us to get, to be honest. We might actually do this."

Lestrade took a sip of his by now lukewarm tea. If he noticed, he gave no indication.

"Who is it?"

"I don't know him," Lestrade said wearily. "We haven't met. But Mr. Williams was certain."

"Lestrade."

"He said it was Inspector. Matthew Flint."

Johnson took a full minute to consider this bit of news. When he finally spoke, it was in little more than a whisper. "Matty Flint. I knew he was crooked, but I always thought he was harmless. I never dreamed…" He ran a hand over his face.

"You're sure?" he demanded.

134

Lestrade sighed. *"I don't know him.* I only know what Mr. Williams said based on a description passed on to me by a stranger who claims he tried to kidnap her daughter."

"We don't have any proof, either way," Johnson said thoughtfully. "I need to talk to Adams and Smith, see what they think about this. Until then, not a word to anyone, Lestrade. And no more independent action, either. I won't overlook it again."

He realized, even as he said it, that Lestrade would listen only to a point. The other man would act as he felt necessary. He could only hope, when it happened again, that Lestrade would be careful, and count the potential danger as well as the reward.

At least, he conceded to himself as he ushered the younger inspector out the door, Lestrade's impromptu and unsanctioned activities had given the man an outlet for his frustration, and having a name and some idea of what needed to be done next had calmed him.

"He needs to learn balance, or he'll burn himself out before very long," Johnson thought as he prepared to go back out himself.

Smith listened to the description Lestrade had given, and Willie's assessment of the identity of the man in question without so much as blinking.

"Could be," he commented when the other man was finished. "Didn't know he was such big fish, but I guess it's possible. Willie's got a memory for names and faces."

Johnson scowled outright. "This complicates things."

"Does it?" Smith asked. "We've been acting as if

anyone at the Yard could be involved. Shouldn't be surprised to find out we're right."

Adams was only slightly more skeptical. "Do we trust the description?" he asked.

"Lestrade felt it had enough merit to be worth pursuing," Johnson pointed out.

"If there's anyone I'd trust to identify someone based off a written description, it's Willie," Adams conceded. "So we believe him, now what?"

Johnson shrugged. "I was thinking about seeing if Willie would talk to me, make sure," he admitted.

Adams snorted. "Good luck."

"Maybe he'll talk to me for Lestrade's sake. He was more friendly with the lad the night of the brawl than I've ever seen him get with anyone, especially a policeman."

Willie scowled at Johnson as soon as he approached the bar. "I've got customers," he growled at the inspector.

Johnson shrugged. "I just came for a drink," he said.

"At the bar, instead of in your usual out-of-the-way corner," Willie pointed out. He served the man anyway.

Johnson, like Lestrade, waited for the bar to close.

"What do ya want?" Willie asked, settling down. "Something happen to young Mr. Lestrade?"

Johnson shook his head. "He was fine, last I saw him. Had some unsettling news."

Willie was suddenly on guard. "Don't know what news you could be talking about, Inspector."

Johnson sighed. "You really think Lestrade's going to

bring down a bunch of slave-traders alone?" he asked.

Willie snorted. "So that's how it is?" he asked.

"Lestrade's not working alone," Johnson told the man. "He needs help, and he's got it. Whether we'll be enough remains to be seen."

Willie shook his head. "Shoulda stayed out of it." After a pause he asked, "What do ya want to know?"

"You're certain about the name?"

"Based on the description given, yes. I've even seen him out and about from time to time, dressed as Lestrade said."

"And the description seems valid?"

"You're asking me?"

"Fair enough. Lestrade thought it worth pursuing, and it was enough to get a name." Johnson grimaced. "Thank you for your time."

Willie shook his head. "Don't go getting that boy killed. He's a good lad, maybe even a good policeman one day."

"One can only hope," Johnson replied dryly.

"We could drop Lestrade in his lap, see what he does," Smith suggested the next morning. "Tell Flint you're busy or tired of him or something, and that no one else will take him. Lestrade can keep his mouth shut, right?"

"Absolutely not." Johnson snapped. "We aren't sending the rookie in to get himself killed. Besides, he's too smart to let anything slip."

"Flint has, up till now, managed to let everyone here think he's involved in nothing more than minor law-breaking." Adams pointed out. "Not likely he'll mess it up now, just because it would be convenient for us."

"Could we follow him? Keep an eye on him somehow?" Smith kept coming up with terrible ideas, but so far he was the only one making suggestions. "Maybe one of our sources could let us know if they see anything suspicious?"

It was Lestrade who shook his head this time. "One person is dead already. Involving others means putting them at risk."

"Couldn't hurt to ask around and see if anyone saw someone matching Flint's description talking to Holdsworth the day he died," Adams said, his voice low. "I'll be back out there anyway, haven't found anything remotely useful in figuring out who murdered him."

Smith looked interested. "You really think it was Matty? He never struck me as the violent sort."

"Did he ever strike you as the sort to be involved in the slave trade?" Adams retorted. "Get me that description, Lestrade, and I'll ask around."

"Be careful." Johnson told him unnecessarily. "In the meantime, we've got more paperwork to sort, don't we Lestrade?"

"Yes, sir."

Johnson wondered whether the other man was beginning to resent being paired with him.

Lestrade looked up as the door opened to reveal an inspector he did not immediately recognize. Johnson had tried to keep him clear of everyone except for Adams and

Smith since they had started investigating the murdered children, only partially out of concern that Lestrade would let something slip, and that only at the beginning.

Johnson had made it clear the rookie was expected to keep quiet and out of the way of the more seasoned inspectors, and that they would come and introduce themselves to *him*, if and when they felt like it.

"Johnson's got you doing busywork, I see." Lestrade looked up at the man suspected of kidnapping and murdering of Henry Abbott and countless other children.

Tall and lanky, with strawberry blonde hair and twinkling hazel eyes, Inspector Matthew Flint — Matty to most of the other Inspectors – looked Lestrade over with a mischievous air that for some reason he could not quite put into words made his blood boil.

"Sir?" Lestrade set aside the files he had been holding and clasped his hands neatly behind his back to hide their shaking.

"They said you were polite." Flint grinned at him. "Polite and quiet. Inspectors like it when the rookie knows how to stay out of the way. I did hear something about you handling yourself in a bar fight on your first day, though, didn't I?"

"Someone hit me with a chair," Lestrade offered, knowing the man expected him to answer.

Flint winced. "Could've been worse. So what do you think of it so far, being an inspector?"

Lestrade looked down at the half empty box of files in front of him and tried for a diplomatic answer. "There seems to be a lot of paperwork."

Diplomacy had never been a strength of his.

Flint laughed outright. "There is, that. And between you and me, Johnson must have his knickers in a twist about something, him dumping you in here like this."

"I don't think he likes me," Lestrade offered the non-answer. To be fair, there had not actually been a question.

"Doesn't matter," Flint replied. "He can't stand Smith, and he still works with him when he has to. Besides, the longer you last, the more likely you'll be accepted by the rest of us. You just have to stick around long enough to prove you're worth it." He looked Lestrade over critically. "And to put a bit of a damper on that youthful enthusiasm."

"Sir?"

Flint laughed. "Never mind, Lestrade. Carry on!" With a jaunty salute he was gone, leaving a scowling Lestrade alone with his files, silently resenting the fact that someone so friendly could do such terrible things.

Lestrade met three more inspectors over the course of the day, each stopping by the back room that was his current assignment and introducing themselves as they looked him over. He made a note of their names and faces, and went back to work when they left.

Johnson sent him home at the end of the day. Lestrade did not argue. Kristina expected him to stop by the grocer on the way home.

It was pure reflex that caused Lestrade to reach out and grab the child's arm when she screamed.

A man dressed in the inexpensive work clothes of the lower class held the girl by her other wrist. He and Lestrade locked eyes, and the younger Inspector knew him immediately.

Flint.

Lestrade lunged forward to put himself between man and child, throwing as much of his weight as he could against Flint's wrist.

The child screamed again. Flint cursed and let go. Turning, he dove into the crowd that was beginning to form. Lestrade debated going after him.

"Get your hands off my child!" Lestrade did not resist the hand that gripped his shoulder and spun him around. "What do you think you're doing?" Lestrade looked up at the large man glaring down at him and considered that he might be in trouble.

The child threw herself at her father. Forced to choose between comforting his daughter and holding on to Lestrade, he released the inspector and knelt down to pull the girl into a hug.

"That man grabbed me," she sobbed, but she was pointing into the distance, not at Lestrade. "He said he had sweets, and puppies, and ribbons."

Her father looked up at Lestrade, perhaps wondering why he had not tried to run. "This man, sweetheart?" he asked, drawing her back to look up at the Inspector.

She shook her head and buried it back in her father's chest.

"I heard her scream," Lestrade offered quietly.

"And just happened to react?" The girl's father was still skeptical.

"I'm a policeman," Lestrade admitted, hating that it

was not the reassurance it should have been. "I worked a case recently that involved a child-snatching. It's been on my mind."

"And when you heard Mary scream, you reacted?" The man was grateful to have his daughter safe, whatever the reason.

Lestrade nodded.

"And you just happened to be here, shopping?"

"I was on my way home from work," Lestrade admitted reluctantly. "I was supposed to stop at the grocer's on my way." He reached for the list neatly folded in his jacket pocket.

"I believe you," the man said, hugging his daughter tightly. "Thank you."

"Couldn't have done anything else." Lestrade murmured. Turning away, he nearly forgot his shopping list as he considered this new development and its consequences.

Johnson eyed his younger counterpart the next morning as the man continued the seemingly never-ending task of straightening out the back room. It was the first time he had seen the man struggle with any of the paperwork he had been assigned.

In truth, Lestrade had been a bit odd since coming in. Not quite jumpy, but certainly not at ease. He was fairly humming with a tension different from any of the frustration Johnson had seen in the man so far in dealing with this slave-traders case.

But Lestrade had not offered an explanation, and so Johnson, not quite ready for whatever trouble he suspected the other man had gotten them into this time, had yet to ask.

It was painfully obvious, however, that for the first time since he had joined them here at the Yard, Lestrade's mind was not at all on the task before him. Johnson had just made up his mind to face reality and ask Lestrade what was bothering him when Matty Flint himself showed up.

"Still got you at work back here?" he asked Lestrade cheerfully. "Are you sure you aren't being punished for something?"

Lestrade's previously distracted air vanished with all the subtlety of a door slamming shut. His eyes, when he looked up in response to the friendly (enough) query, were painfully blank.

"Sir?" Johnson was certain by now that the response was an evasion tactic. Flint chuckled and shifted his attention to the older man.

"We met yesterday," he told Johnson. "He was in a different corner of the room then. He seems polite enough."

"Infuriatingly so, at times," Johnson replied, trying to ignore the shiver running down his spine. Really, Flint was the last person anyone would ever suspect of being involved in as slave-trafficking ring. Johnson himself looked far more suspicious, and Lestrade…

If he didn't know better he could easily suspect Lestrade of heading up just about any crime ring, going on looks alone.

No wonder the man worked so hard to dress and sound respectable.

"Thought I saw you down on Market Street yesterday, Lestrade. Could've sworn you saw me, but you kept on walking."

The younger inspector only shrugged. "I might have been a bit distracted," he admitted. "I was thinking about how nice it would be to have my own office."

It was a lie, and a terribly unconvincing one at that. Johnson could see it plainly in the other man's eyes, but Flint either wasn't looking, or didn't know Lestrade well enough to know better.

Flint excused himself after that, claiming plans to meet another inspector for lunch. The flippant salute he offered Lestrade was reassuring. Maybe he just wanted to get to know the new inspector a bit. Maybe he didn't know they were on to him.

Lestrade remained frozen stiffly in place even after the man had left. When he finally moved, it was let out a long, heartfelt sigh of relief that did nothing to lessen any of the tension in his shoulders.

Johnson considered all this carefully. "Maybe we should take a break," he suggested.

Back in Johnson's office with the door locked, Lestrade did not need to be prompted to share the details of his meeting with Flint the previous day, or his introductions to Inspectors Crane, Craddock, and Garrett. Johnson tried to brush off any concern, knowing that by now Lestrade had been around long enough that it was only natural for the other inspectors to start showing some interest in him. If all four inspectors happened to be suspected of involvement in less than legal goings on, the older Inspector was forced to admit that very few policemen at the Yard currently were not.

He was more concerned with Lestrade's subsequent retelling of the events of the previous evening, at the market where Flint had claimed he had seen the other Inspector.

"He's testing you," Johnson said. "Maybe to see if you recognized him. Or if you were going to tell anyone. He may be waiting to see if you're going to cause trouble."

He frowned. Whatever the reason for Flint's visit today, Lestrade was likely in very real danger. Whether or not he would survive it was yet to be seen.

Twelve

After Lestrade's news, Johnson was almost afraid to let the younger man out of his sight. He fully intended to shuffle him off into the back room once more and keep him there for the remainder of the evening, but news of a man being struck down by a cab dragged them out into the comparatively unprotected streets of London that afternoon.

There was nothing suspicious about the death; a man, far too drunk for the time of day and long in the habit of being so (according to a few onlookers who recognized him), had staggered out of the pub and into the street without bothering to look around him before stepping right into the path of a cab that unfortunately did not expect him, and did not see him in time to stop.

It was a straightforward if tragic affair, and quickly dealt with. The only thing of note was the easy way in which Lestrade interacted with the still highly nervous cab horse; while the other policemen had been reluctant to get anywhere near the animal while it still carried the scent of blood in its nostrils, Lestrade had wasted no time in approaching it, stroking its head and mumbling words that quickly began to take effect. By the time the shaken cab driver had come back to himself the creature was calm enough, if still nervous.

Lestrade was talking horses with the man when Johnson finished up, but he had also gotten a fairly accurate account from the driver concerning the incident.

The rest of the day was spent on paperwork; even without a murder there were still forms to complete and people to be notified. Johnson figured that if the other man had been previously unaware of the sheer amount of filing that went with the promotion to inspector, it was a misconception that had been rapidly corrected during their time together.

He resisted the urge to escort the man home. Lestrade was not an errant child, and such behavior would only serve to draw more unwanted attention. He sent the younger inspector off with an admonition to be careful, and set off for home himself.

Careful or not, Lestrade was not fully prepared for the bullet that whizzed past his shoulder and shattered the wall behind him. Ducking into the alley, he darted into the shadows and looked around almost frantically.

The bullet had come from above, but nobody lingered in open windows for him to locate. The shooter was gone. More pressing, Lestrade realized abruptly that he was not alone.

He made a break for it, lunging back in the direction he had just come, only to find his way blocked by a man nearly twice his size.

Two more men approached Lestrade from behind while he considered his situation.

He threw a punch, hitting the man squarely in the jaw, and turned abruptly, lunging to the left of the men coming up behind him, hoping to catch them off guard. It nearly worked; Lestrade dodged around them to find himself staring into a dead end.

Lestrade swore under his breath and turned to face his

assailants. Outnumbered, he braced himself for a unfair fight with no delusions of winning.

Light glinted off metal as one of the men drew a blade, and Lestrade realized that he was in for more than just a beating – these men fully intended to kill him.

Lestrade threw himself at the man who was currently brandishing a knife at him with little hope for an outcome that would not leave him bleeding out in the alley. The man lunged; Lestrade barely managed to avoid being stabbed.

If all three of them had attacked at once, Lestrade would never have stood a chance. As it was, the other two man held back, watching, confident in the armed man's ability to make short work of the new inspector.

Lestrade turned, kicking his assailant in the knee. His foot connected with a not entirely unsatisfying crunch, and the man went down screaming. He dropped the knife, but before Lestrade could consider retrieving it the larger of the two remaining men let out a roar and charged at him.

Lestrade went down hard and rolled, knowing that to stop even for a moment could prove fatal. He came back up, fists raised, ignoring his body as it protested in several different places.

The man simply picked him up and slammed him into a wall. For a moment the world went out of focus and threatened to go dark. Lestrade shook his head, remembered to breathe, and reached for the hands pinning him against dirty brick, fingers searching desperately for tender spots. His left thumb found a spot and dug in. The man's grip wavered, and Lestrade's right found another.

He realized the man had lifted him several feet off the

ground only as the impact of landing made him stumble. Cursing, he threw an off balance punch at the other man that did little more than make him angrier than he already was.

The third of Lestrade's attackers moved in, realizing that Lestrade was not as easy a target as they had initially thought. Lestrade saw him out of the corner of his eye as he narrowly avoided being grabbed again and quickly considered his options.

He was now between the two men and the street. The man he had most likely crippled by breaking his knee was still on the ground. The other two men were still standing, both with a clear advantage when it came to size and a strong desire to kill the man in front of them.

Out of breath, outnumbered, and more than slightly dizzy from where the back of his head had hit the brick wall, Lestrade knew full well it was only due to overconfidence on the part of his attackers that he was not already dead.

Personal pride or not, Lestrade was fully capable of admitting his limitations. He had no chance against these two men, and he had no interest in being the next body laid out on the pavement. He turned and ran, darting straight into the street itself and narrowly avoiding being struck by more than one driver, ignoring the angry swearing he provoked as he did so.

Lestrade turned down one street, then another, finally ducking into an alley and crouching into the shadows in the hopes of being overlooked. His breath coming in short, shallow gasps, Lestrade waited. After several minutes, he straightened up and risked moving forward to eye the street carefully. He saw no sign of his attackers.

Lestrade gradually became aware of a throbbing in his upper arm that was accompanied by a hot, wet sensation. Looking down, he realized that his knife-wielding assailant had managed to slice open his arm before he went down.

Shaking his head to clear it and reaching for a handkerchief that was not likely to be up to the task, Lestrade wondered if it were safe to go home.

Looking down at his arm, he frowned and made up his mind. His right arm was still bleeding, and there was no way he could stitch it up himself left-handed. He was not overly worried about putting his sister in danger; Kristina was far more capable of handling herself than most people realized. Any man looking for trouble was likely to meet up with one of her kitchen knives – most likely the one she used to fillet fish – before he even realized what was happening.

Johnson did not like the way Adams and Smith flanked him as he headed toward his office the following morning. It was too overt, too obvious to anyone who happened to see them that the three inspectors were collaborating on something. Given the nature of said collaboration, being seen together like this was downright dangerous, and both men knew it.

They followed Johnson into his office, where Lestrade, as was usual for him, already waited. The second he caught sight of the younger man, Johnson understood.

He jerked his head toward the door, and Smith closed it. He and Adams proceeded to take over the available seating while Johnson moved in to get a better look at the younger inspector.

Lestrade had clearly taken a beating since Johnson had last seen him. The man stood ill at ease, holding himself carefully as if the simple act of breathing might overwhelm him. His right arm was cradled almost protectively against his side, as if to keep from jostling it. His expression was pinched, framed in a too pale face and eyes that fairly glittered with some unidentified emotion.

"What happened?" Johnson kept his voice low, both to keep from being overheard and, hopefully, to keep from spooking the injured man standing before him. He could not yet read Lestrade well enough to tell whether the man were seriously injured, and there was something in the man's eyes that worried him.

"Someone almost shot me on my way home," Lestrade sounded frustrated rather than frightened. Johnson was not sure that was a good thing. "I ducked into an alley to find three men waiting for me. One of them sliced open my arm. Another shoved me into a brick wall."

"And you got away?" Adams demanded. Smith looked impressed.

Lestrade offered a one-shouldered shrug. "They waited. The second only came to help after I broke the first one's knee. His friend took even longer to join in."

"You'd be dead now if they'd all attacked at once," Johnson suggested. Lestrade did not deny it. He was well aware of the fact.

"When the opportunity presented itself, I ran," he admitted. "Even with just the two of them I was outmatched."

"Flint must have realized you recognized him after

all," Johnson decided. "Adams, let the rookie sit." Eyeing Lestrade, he added, "That's not a suggestion."

Adams shrugged, and the younger man reluctantly took his place. "Does he know about the rest of us, though?" Smith wondered.

"He has to by now, the way you two were acting when I came in," Johnson pointed out. "Either way, we need to act, and act fast."

"And do what?" Adams wanted to know. "We don't have anything against him but Lestrade's word, and you know how far that will go here."

"But we know it's him." Smith looked thoughtful. "Maybe we could *find* some actual proof."

"We can't search his office," Johnson felt compelled to remind the man.

"No, but that likely wouldn't do any good anyway. I doubt he takes the missing children here after he takes them."

"We can't search his house, either," Adams all but growled.

"But we could watch him," Smith pointed out. "No harm in looking. Maybe he'll even lead us to some of his friends. A big enough arrest, and even the superintendent can't ignore it."

Johnson felt his mouth go dry. They were in way over their heads. "You must be mad. There's only three of us."

"Four," Smith countered. "And anyway, Lestrade got in the way of his last attempt. The question is whether he was out hunting, or whether it was a crime of opportunity."

"He was dressed like a lower-class workman when he

tried to grab the girl." Lestrade's voice was carefully neutral.

"Do you think he'll try again soon?" Adams asked. Out of the three older inspectors, Smith had the most experience dealing with actual policemen-turned-criminal.

"The Abbot boy was taken fairly recently," Smith pointed out. "When he died, Flint wasted little time in looking for a replacement. He failed that time too."

"So you think he'll try again soon?" Johnson asked. "Even after Lestrade stopped him?"

"If someone's expecting him to deliver, he may not be able to wait," Adams realized. "He may be pressed for time. Or money. Or he may feel pressured, in light of his recent failures, to prove himself."

"He hasn't been successful so far," Johnson felt obligated to mention. "Four, five dead children in how many months, and this last one got away from him completely."

"Exactly," Smith grinned. "He may be getting desperate. So we put a tail on him." He turned to eye Lestrade thoughtfully. "He'd fit in with the lower class well enough, once we got him out of that suit."

"Absolutely not!" Johnson snapped. "He's been on the job less than a week. Flint will kill him if he's caught."

Smith shrugged. "He already tried yesterday. I doubt he'd even notice Lestrade, as long as he didn't look him in the eye."

Johnson was not going to lose this argument. Turning to Lestrade, he asked, "Do you actually have any experience working undercover? Or tailing people?" The man frowned, but shook his head. "That's what I thought. Smith, you're plenty experienced in both areas. So is Adams, for that

153

matter. One of you – or both, if you prefer – can tail Flint's movements after he leaves here, and report back if you learn anything of interest. It would be foolish to send in an inspector with barely a week of experience in when the two of you have already been trained to the work."

Smith had to agree. He and Adams agreed to take turns tailing the man.

"One other thing," Adams felt obligated to point out. "There's only four of us. We need help. Is there anyone else we can trust with this?"

Johnson resisted the urge to sigh. The sad truth of the matter was that the three men currently in his office were the only inspectors at the Yard he would trust with this sort of thing, and before they had gotten themselves involved, he hadn't even been sure of Smith or Adams.

Smith scowled. "Craddock would do it."

Adams stared at him. "*Craddock?* Are you mad? The man is a monster."

"He has a soft spot for children," Smith argued. "He doesn't like slave-traders either."

"Everyone *knows* he's dirty, though," Johnson countered. "Flint could use his involvement against us, he's clever enough. He'd go free and we'd be that much worse off."

Lestrade cleared his throat. Shifting uneasily in his seat, he did not look up as he spoke. "Constable Gregory is clean. Collins and Andrews too."

"Your friends from Fleet Street?" Adams asked. Lestrade nodded. The older inspector looked at Johnson. "They're constables. I met them on that case where the woman was thrown out of a window."

Johnson frowned. "Can they handle themselves in a fight, if it comes to it?" he asked. "I'm not interested in getting constables killed." Lestrade nodded again.

"And you'd trust them with this?" Adams pressed.

"I'd trust Gregory with my life," Lestrade replied. Cautiously, he continued, "He's better at turning a blind eye when he knows there's not much he can do, but he's honest. The other two are young and idealistic and hoping to make a difference."

Johnson felt his eyebrows raise. "You get a lot of those, over on Fleet Street?"

Lestrade shrugged, but answered anyway. "Collins and Andrews won't last."

Johnson wondered whether his attempted murder had rattled him more than he let on. He did not seem to be filtering his answers quite as much today.

"*Too* idealistic?" Adams challenged. "What about you? You seem to lean a bit too far that way yourself, Lestrade. Either that, or you're far too naive for a man who's been on the force for as long as you claim."

Lestrade did look up then. "I'm not blind," he told the older inspector shortly. "I know right from wrong, and just because something's come to be accepted, doesn't make it right."

"But they can handle themselves in a fight?" Johnson asked again, before Adams could reply.

"They can," Lestrade confirmed.

Three days passed with agonizing slowness. Smith,

taking the first day, learned nothing. Flint left Scotland Yard, stopped at Willie's for a drink, then went home, remaining there through the night. Adams, taking the second day, endured the same tedious sort of evening. When Smith took the third day things went more or less exactly the same, with the exception that Flint took dinner at Willie's before heading home.

Meanwhile, Lestrade threw himself back into reorganizing the papers in the back room with an enthusiasm that was almost alarming. The room already looked better than Johnson could ever remember, and the man was only about halfway finished. Lestrade had a knack for organization, something that far too many inspectors at the Yard currently lacked.

On the fourth evening, just as Johnson was about to send Lestrade home for the night and hope for better luck tomorrow, a runner came with a message from Adams.

Flint was on the move.

He had left his flat and hailed a cab, giving an address down by the docks. They were to wait for further updates.

The next half hour went by at an infuriating crawl. Smith was pacing the small room, getting in everyone's way. Lestrade no longer even pretended to be reading the file in his hands. Johnson tried not to calculate the possibilities of getting through the night alive.

An hour after the first message, word came to move out.

Johnson had his misgivings about including Lestrade

in the night's activities. Never mind that he had started all this. Never mind that he had previously demonstrated the ability to hold his own in a fight. He was still too new to all this. Still far too untried. It was irresponsible, and Johnson knew it.

Getting three constables involved, no matter how willing, was even worse.

There were, however, only seven of them, rookie inspector and constables included. They did not have the luxury of depositing Lestrade somewhere safe for the night. They could not afford to send the constables home. Adams and Smith were both capable enough men. Johnson himself was no stranger to trouble. But the fact remained that even with Lestrade, they were only seven men.

Adams was waiting for them outside the warehouse. Holding a finger to his lips in warning, he eased open the door. The other men followed.

Inside was dark and dirty. A light glimmered faintly in one corner, and voices drifted faintly through the air. Someone was angry, another defensive. An argument, then.

Six men were seated around a table, one filthy lamp offering its solitary light to the gathering from its place of honor in the center. Flint was among them. Johnson recognized several of the others; they had stumbled upon hardened criminals.

Upon seeing the other inspectors, he swore and leaped to his feet. His companions followed, and in the next moment, Johnson was fighting for his life.

Lestrade took one look at the knife his opponent

currently held and reconsidered his situation. He had little interest in being cut open again. Too many encounters with knives lately.

A discarded chair stood between them. Lestrade took a step forward and kicked the chair, sending it crashing right into the other man's legs. For whatever reason, the man was not ready to deal with such an assault and stumbled, cursing as he dropped his weapon.

Lestrade closed the distance between them before the man could recover the blade, but quickly realized the fight was far from over. His opponent was more than capable of using his fists as well.

Lestrade was reminded that they were outnumbered when he was forced to dodge an attack from the side. In the meantime, his original target managed to land a punch that set his head ringing.

Lestrade ducked down and forward, landing a blow to the man's chest that knocked the wind out of him. He doubled over, gasping, only to backhand Lestrade when he moved in closer.

Out of the corner of his eye Lestrade saw someone throw a chair. Someone else was crashing into the table, knocking the lamp over. Lestrade somehow managed to avoid being hit a third time and threw a punch that connected solidly with his opponent's nose.

He turned just in time to see Adams go down. Someone had retrieved the dropped knife. Carefully Lestrade eased up behind the man as he stood over the wounded inspector. A quick blow to the back of the head sent the man to his knees.

The fight was over quickly enough. Adams received the worst of the injuries on their side, having been stabbed in the shoulder. Of their enemies, one lay still upon the ground, dead.

Lestrade was certain he did not want to know who had killed him.

The rest of the men were handcuffed and warned against further resistance, but the loss of their companion seemed to have taken the fight out of them.

A quick search of the building revealed a locked room upstairs. Smith, having used up his store of patience for the evening, kicked it open, scaring several small children and one young lady who looked to be nearly fourteen.

He spent several long, unsuccessful minutes trying to get them to calm down before giving up and sticking his head back through the doorway to call for reinforcements. Johnson, busy tending to Adams's shoulder, sent Lestrade to help while the constables kept an eye on their prisoners.

Smith was left staring as Lestrade took one look around the room before immediately scooping the youngest of the children off the ground and propping it against his waist with little regard for its current, bedraggled state. He was even more surprised when the child stopped crying.

"You're safe now," he told the others. Looking at the other two children, he raised an eyebrow. "You're both big enough to walk now, aren't you?" he asked, his tone far gentler than the other inspector had ever heard it. "Brave enough too, I wouldn't wonder." Looking the older of the two over critically, he nodded in satisfaction. "I'm sure a fine young man like yourself is capable of helping the young lady down the stairs?"

If the boy was only five, and the young lady in question much more likely to be helping him, the fact did not seem to occur to him as he went over to the girl and offered her his hand. The young lady, tired and frightened but hardly a fool, smiled and did not mention it.

Lestrade considered the other boy. "You can help Inspector Smith down the stairs, if you will. He took a blow to the head earlier, and I fear he may still be a bit addled."

Smith chuckled, but allowed the boy to take his hand. He would not have expected Lestrade to have a way with children, but the man seemed to be far more comfortable with these little ones than his fellow policemen.

They rejoined the others downstairs, children in tow. Johnson stared outright at Lestrade and his small bundle, who had, in fact, latched tightly to his jacket and gave no indication of ever letting go.

Lestrade did not seem to notice the resulting wrinkles.

Johnson looked around. "Gregory, send word that we need to transport these men back to the Yard. Smith, the other two constables can help you get loaded up while Lestrade finds out who the children are. The sooner we get them back home, the better."

"I can help with that, sir," the young lady spoke up, her voice trembling slightly. "And I can help watch them until their parents come."

"Thank you," Johnson said. The girl would do better with something to keep her occupied. "Adams, you sit still and be quiet. You're lucky they only got your arm."

Adams glared at him, but did not argue.

Adams recovered from his knife wound, though neither injury nor illness ever seemed to keep the man down for long. He would still favor that shoulder a month later, at least when the weather was damp, but that was only to be expected.

Lestrade was unceremoniously moved out of Johnson's office and into what used to be Flint's. He was also left with the dubious honor of cleaning out the man's belongings, but predictably never complained. Johnson was delighted to have his own office to himself again.

Lestrade's first official case turned out to be far less exciting than dealing with slave-traders, but the man hardly seemed to mind. If anything, he seemed to appreciate the comparatively simple case, wherein a man shot his wife in front of no less than three witnesses, leaving Lestrade with little more to do than arrest him and spend the remainder of the day dealing with the resulting paperwork. The man seemed to be settling into his role as Detective Inspector Lestrade, and he appeared to be doing a good job at it.

Johnson looked around Lestrade's new office. The room was neat, organized, everything he would have expected of the man based on their time together. Lestrade sat behind his desk, filling out some form or another – really, the paperwork never ended – looking somehow as if he belonged there.

"Happy?" he asked, inviting himself into the chair opposite the other man.

Lestrade blinked at him uncertainly. "Sir?"

Johnson rolled his eyes. "You did good work, this week. Solid police work. Took on an issue everyone else was content to ignore." He paused.

Lestrade did not seem inclined to comment. A moment later, Johnson continued.

"They found the whole gang guilty. Flint's going to hang."

"I heard." It was nearly impossible to tell how the younger man felt about that. Truthfully, Johnson didn't know how he felt about it himself. He was still trying to process the fact that Matty Flint had been guilty of abducting children for his less than savory partners to sell.

Johnson realized Lestrade was staring at him and cleared his throat.

"Just don't let it go to your head, and we might make a decent inspector out of you yet," he said.

Lestrade shrugged, uncomfortable at the frank praise. "I'll try not to, sir."

Also from Orange Pip Books

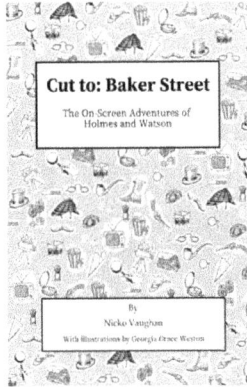

Cut to: Baker Street
The On-Screen Adventures of
Holmes and Watson

By
Nicko Vaughan
With Illustrations by Georgia Grace Weston

It is well documented that Sherlock Holmes is the most depicted literary character on screen; he even has an entry in the Guinness Book of Records to prove it. This reference guide covers depictions of the world's most famous detective, and his faithful companion, from the first silent film Sherlock Holmes is Baffled (1900) to the Will Ferrell, John C. Reilly comedy Holmes and Watson (2018). As well as cinema and television portrayals, this book by Nicko Vaughan (Author of The Wordy Companion: An A-Z Guide to Sherlockian Phraseology) also covers documentaries, animations and web series adaptations alongside début feature artwork by graphic artist Georgia Grace Weston.

Combining encyclopaedia, biography and reference structure, this book comprehensively explores the many celluloid faces, cathode-ray shapes and digital sizes of Sherlock Holmes and Doctor John Watson, so far.

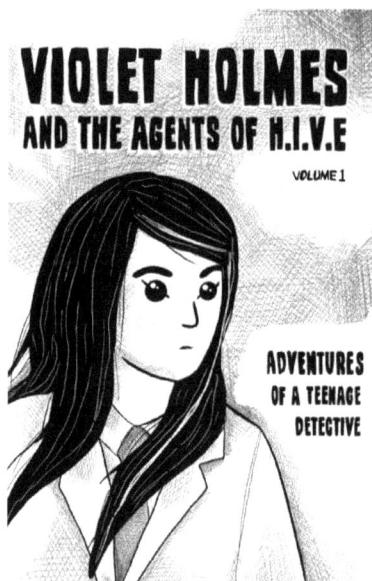

VIOLET HOLMES
AND THE AGENTS OF H.I.V.E
VOLUME 1

ADVENTURES
OF A TEENAGE
DETECTIVE

Violet Holmes is not an ordinary teenager because, well, nothing is ordinary when you're the adopted daughter of the great Sherlock Holmes. Having been home schooled for her entire life she has decided to take the plunge, at 14, and attend Bardle Secondary School to study for her exams. But after a week, she notices that the school hides a deep secret, and she's determined to crack it wide open. Are the current spate of school thefts the work of criminal masterminds? Is there really a secret society behind closed doors? Can a girl like Violet make friends and fit in?

Also from Orange Pip Books

Just the place for a Nark!" the Detective cried,
As he eagerly surveyed the scene;
With the stout-hearted Doctor alert at his side,
And the Dog standing guard in between.

Imagine a world where the logic of Sherlock Holmes meets the nonsense of Wonderland! *The Hunting of the Nark* combines the best of Lewis Carroll and Arthur Conan Doyle's adventures into a madcap collection of verse, including the novella-length case, *The Adventure of the Twinkling Hat*. Holmes and Watson will discover that anything can happen at 221B when you're the White Knight...

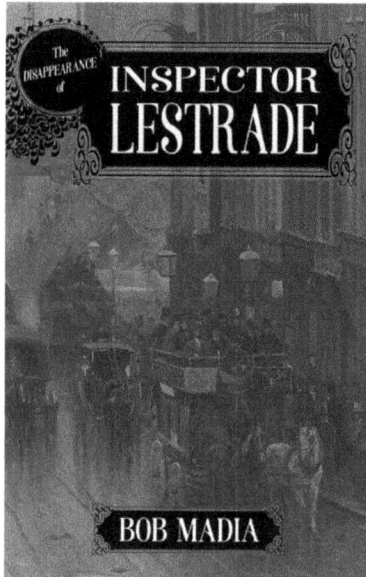

Dr. John H. Watson is a man of medical science, a man of action and a man of letters. His life has been one of adventure and romance. In 1894 he finds himself alone following the death of his great friend Sherlock Holmes three years earlier and now the passing of his beloved wife, Mary. His loneliness is all encompassing and only a true friend can help him to see there is still reason to continue living. But when that friend, Inspector G. Lestrade of Scotland Yard suddenly and mysteriously disappears, Dr. Watson takes it upon himself to discover the reason for the abduction.

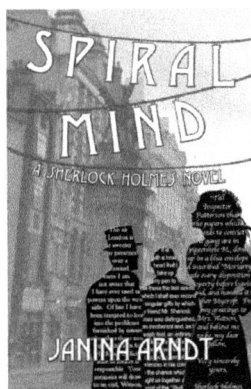

It wasn't that John couldn't tell the story. It wasn't that we didn't know the truth. It was that nobody would believe us. But we cannot keep Sherlock alive with silence. The reader smiles when Moriarty appears on the page. So does Moriarty. And Sherlock Holmes follows him. We smile because we recognise them. Scarlett Vendalle is recognised by nobody, except for John Watson. With no recollection of her own identity and a suspected criminal past, Scarlett is the perfect case for Sherlock. As they follow her tracks, red threads appear in their lives that make it more than clear - Scarlett meeting John and Sherlock was no coincidence. Someone has drawn her shadow on the wall before she appeared. Was it Anne Boleyn who haunts Scarlett with visions of her past? Was it Moriarty who attracts Sherlock like a magnet? Or was it another shadow from the past? With Moriarty's men on the one hand and the secret service on the other, the stage is set for a game with deadly rules, as Sherlock, John and Scarlett slowly become aware that something larger is guiding their steps... Is there another story being written...?